THE CHAIN

50 YEARS OF FLEETWOOD MAC

Written by
PETE CHRISP

Danann
BOOKS

© Danann Publishing Limited 2017

First Published Danann Publishing Ltd 2017

WARNING: For private domestic use only, any unauthorised Copying, hiring, lending or public performance of this book is illegal.

CAT NO: DAN0362

Photography courtesy of

Getty images:

Michael Ochs Archives / Stringer	Richard E. Aaron/Redferns	Noam Galai
GAB Archive	Julian Wasser/The LIFE Images Collection	Kevin Kane
Michael Putland	Paul Natkin	Neilson Barnard
GAB Archive/Redferns	Frans Schellekens/Redferns	George Wilkes/Hulton Archive
Bob Baker/Redferns	The LIFE Picture Collection	Ed Perlstein/Redferns
George Wilkes/Hulton Archive	Donna Santisi/Redferns	Brian Rasic
Fin Costello/Redferns	Hulton Archive	Michael Putland
Jay L. Clendenin	Tim Mosenfelder	
Richard McCaffrey/Michael Ochs Archives	Martin Philbey/Redferns	

Book layout & design Darren Grice at Ctrl-d

Made in EU.

ISBN: 978-1-912332-09-0

CONTENTS

4   PROLOGUE: BEHIND THE MASK An introduction to Fleetwood Mac

6   CHAPTER 1:   ENGLISH ROSE The British blues boom and the birth of Fleetwood Mac

10   CHAPTER 2:   MR WONDERFUL Peter Green's Fleetwood Mac

20   CHAPTER 3:   BARE TREES Fleetwood Mac's wilderness years, Part 1

28   CHAPTER 4:   HEROES ARE HARD TO FIND Will the real Fleetwood Mac please stand up

36   CHAPTER 5:   RUMOURS Fleetwood Mac's perfect relationships

50   CHAPTER 6:   FROM TUSK TO TANGO Fleetwood Mac's changes in direction

58   CHAPTER 7:   FROM TANGO TO TIME Fleetwood Mac's wilderness years, Part 2

66   CHAPTER 8:   SAY YOU WILL Fleetwood Mac born again

76   EPILOGUE: FUTURE GAMES Where now for Fleetwood Mac?

80   BIOGRAPHIES

88   STUDIO ALBUMS

108   COMPILATIONS AND LIVE ALBUMS

110   ACKNOWLEDGEMENTS AND SOURCES

ABOUT THE AUTHOR

PETE CHRISP has worked as a writer and editor for newspapers, magazines and books since 1979.
His first book, co-written with the musician Gerry McAvoy, was the highly acclaimed *Riding Shotgun: 35 Years on the Road with Rory Gallagher and Nine Below Zero*. He lives in Kent, England.

PROLOGUE:
BEHIND THE MASK
AN INTRODUCTION TO FLEETWOOD MAC

ALL ROCK BANDS ARE UNIQUE, ONE WAY OR ANOTHER, BUT NO OTHER ROCK BAND IS QUITE AS UNIQUE AS FLEETWOOD MAC.

For 50 years they have entertained, enthralled, shocked, amused and amazed the world — all stemming from a little British blues band which, back in 1967, never expected, or even wanted, to be anything more than just that.

Within two years they had become something much bigger. Their first album, *Fleetwood Mac*, rose to No. 4 in the UK charts. Their third single 'Black Magic Woman', written by band leader Peter Green, went on to become a huge worldwide hit for Santana. Their fifth single, 'Albatross', topped the UK charts; their next two singles, 'Man of the World' and 'Oh Well' both made it to No. 2.

This was a band going somewhere fast, often outselling even the Beatles. Then, on the verge of worldwide recognition, Peter Green — uncomfortable at such a height of success, both artistically and financially — bailed out, leaving the band lost and rudderless. Their choice was either to quit, or start again. Fleetwood Mac never quit, even when maybe they should have.

For the next five years they sailed through troubled waters, changing their line-up no less than five times, flapping in panic beneath the surface. Band members came and went on a regular basis; some (quite literally) disappeared. No one ever just 'left' Fleetwood Mac; instead, band members got sucked into religious cults; had affairs with other people's partners; or threw wobblers and got sacked.

But, somehow, they made it to as far as 1975 to reach a turning point no one could have predicted. Two unknown folk pop musicians from California arrived at their doorstep and helped transform a trio of British blues rockers into one of the biggest bands in the world.

No one knew what was just around the corner in 1977, or the pain and heartache they would go through to create it. *Rumours*: one of the best LPs ever and, at one stage, the best selling album of all time, which would continue to sell, and sell, and sell, for the next 40 years, shifting more than 40million copies.

To top it was impossible, so they didn't even try. Instead they threw their hat in the ring with punk and produced an album nobody liked. *Tusk*. Another downward spiral began. No other band has experienced artistic peaks and troughs or emotional highs and lows quite like Fleetwood Mac. And no other band has maintained such intense, long-term, audience interest in their musical — and personal — development.

They've never been as cool as the Rolling Stones or Led Zeppelin; never as influential as the Beatles or Jimi Hendrix; never as well-respected as Pink Floyd or the Allman Brothers Band; but after 50 years on the road, Fleetwood Mac are still going strong, still performing and still winning over new audiences across the world.

WELCOME TO A LONG STORY SHORT OF ROCK 'N' ROLL'S GREATEST EVER SOAP OPERA.

PETE CHRISP MAY 2017

RIGHT

Fleetwood Mac board their private jet, circa 1975

CHAPTER 1:

ENGLISH ROSE

THE BRITISH BLUES BOOM AND THE BIRTH OF FLEETWOOD MAC

Think about the 1960s in the UK, whether you lived through that period or not, and the first images that spring to mind are paisley shirts and kipper ties, mini-skirts and Mini cars, Chelsea boots and hippie sandals, the Beatles and the Stones, Mods and Rockers and England swinging like a pendulum-do. Those happy days now seem so very long ago but were understandable for a country that had gone through six years of shortages, misery and hardship during World War II followed by more than a decade of economic austerity, food rations and racial discrimination.

Harold Macmillan's famous declaration that "most of our people have never had it so good" came in July 1957 at a time when the country was riding high on the post-war economic boom that would lead to the UK's defining Swinging Sixties. But something else took place in the late '50s and early '60s that's not so easy to explain: the British blues boom, or explosion, that crept in through the back door, many believe as a direct result of World War II.

There's little doubt that the UK would not have defeated Nazi Germany without the help of over 3million troops from the British Commonwealth and more than 16million troops from the USA, around 3million of whom found themselves stationed across the UK — from Belfast to Glasgow, Newcastle to Birmingham, Liverpool to London, Cardiff to Southampton — and of which, more than 100,000 soldiers and sailors were black.

Britain's black resident population in the 1940s was less than 20,000 and, for most of the American servicemen sailing to the UK, it would be their first experience of life on foreign soil. Many were nervous as to how they'd be received in the UK, expecting still to be subjected to racial segregation as happened in America. They were prepared to live and pass their time-off

in British black ghettos by bringing their own entertainment — often their collections of blues and jazz records.

In truth, most black servicemen were welcomed with open arms in the UK and many British troops and civilians stood shoulder to shoulder with them to defend their rights against racial segregation and abuse from white American GIs, many of whom wanted blacks banned from using British pubs, clubs and cinemas. Punch-ups, protests and even riots took place on a regular basis on Saturday nights.

When the time came for black troops to head off to France as part of the D-Day invasion, most had no choice but to offload their records, some as thank-you gifts but many sold to record shops and market stalls to raise funds before heading off into an uncertain future.

Thus, according to urban folklore, virtually unheard of blues and jazz music began to drip-feed its way through British culture over the next decade. In reality, there had already been some interest in blues and jazz music in the UK since the 1930s, with US stars such as Bessie Smith, Billie Holiday, Fats Waller and Jelly Roll Morton gaining a British audience and selling records on UK labels in specialist stores.

Big band swing music from the likes of Glenn Miller, Duke Ellington, Tommy Dorsey and Count Basie dominated the '40s and '50s until rock 'n' roll was launched in 1955, when Bill Haley and His Comets shot to No. 1 in the USA and UK with 'Rock Around the Clock'. But rock 'n' roll wasn't the only music of the '50s. By the latter years, Bill Haley had had his day, Elvis was in the US Army, Buddy Holly was dead, Little Richard had given it up to become a preacher and Chuck Berry was fighting a prison sentence; as a result, the charts tended to be full of rather tepid, feel-good crooners such as Perry Como, Pat Boone and Bing Crosby.

Such sounds may well have represented the innocence of post World War II optimism in America, but new stars in the UK — the likes of Cliff Richard and Billy Fury — lacked the excitement and energy that Elvis and Bill Haley had stirred in teenagers; and UK youngsters needed something to give music a kick-start. The result had an equally dramatic impact on British '50s teenagers: skiffle.

Just like punk, skiffle was a simple form of music that anyone could have a go at, whether they played an instrument well or not. As long as someone could sing and play a few chords on a cheap acoustic guitar, or even a banjo, background rhythms could be bashed out on a beaten up piano, with a stringed broom handle and tea chest for a bass and a washboard for the drums. Cheap, cheerful but highly effective and hugely popular.

Across the UK, thousands of skiffle bands were formed and began to perform at school dances, church halls and coffee bars; many famous British musicians began their careers just that way — most notably John Lennon's band the Quarrymen, who recruited Paul and George in 1957 and went on to become the Beatles.

Guitarist and banjo player Lonnie Donegan led the skiffle revolution, with no less than 28 Top 30 singles in the UK, initially as part of trombonist Chris Barber's Jazz Band — one of the biggest names in the UK trad-jazz scene along with Acker Bilk and Kenny Ball. Such was its success that the London Skiffle Club was opened in 1955 at the Roundhouse pub in Soho and run by two musicians, Cyril Davies and Alexis Korner, both of whom had also worked for Chris Barber.

Just like rock 'n' roll, however, skiffle began to decline towards the end of the '50s, so much so that Chris Barber decided to concentrate on bringing over more American blues artists who had been finding it difficult to make a living in America. Blues music was probably too much of a reminder to many Americans as to where this music had come from — African-Americans, who had been given their freedom but very little else. There was no audience for them in the USA but, in the UK, they couldn't get enough.

Big Bill Broonzy was the first big name Chris Barber brought over, followed by the likes of Memphis Slim, Champion Jack Dupree and Sonny Terry & Brownie McGhee, playing mainly acoustic and country blues sets which became so successful that Cyril Davies and Alexis Korner eventually closed their Skiffle Club and opened the London Blues and Barrelhouse Club at the same venue in Soho.

In 1958 an event took place at the club that is reputed to have had a major impact on UK blues: Muddy Waters used electric amplifiers to play there at such a high level of volume that Davies and Korner were completely blown away. Inspired and ahead of the game yet again, they formed a new band, Blues Incorporated, that not only attempted to match Muddy's electric energy levels but also became a boot camp for British blues musicians over the next few years. Many of them would go on to become the future Rolling Stones, Yardbirds, Cream, Kinks, Animals, Manfred Mann… It was the first British blues boom. Or perhaps even an explosion!

The explosion took place across the UK but the truth was that, to make it to the top, you needed to be in London. That was the advice given by Alexis Korner to another British musician, John Mayall, in a Manchester band called Blues Syndicate who would often support Blues Incorporated in northern England. At the age of almost 30, Mayall was no spring chicken and so decided to take Korner's advice. It was a good move; by 1963, Mayall's new band, the Bluesbreakers, had a residency at London's Marquee Club and became another fluid finishing school for British blues musicians including: Jack Bruce, Aynsley Dunbar, Eric Clapton, Keef Hartley, Andy Fraser, Mick Taylor… and three young men called Peter Green, Mick Fleetwood and John McVie. It was the second British blues boom… and the future Fleetwood Mac.

Peter Green (born Greenbaum into a devout Jewish family in the East End of London) had taken up guitar aged 10 or 11 during the skiffle period and played in various London bands but his real love was the blues, especially American guitarist BB King; that was the sort of music he wanted to play. At that stage the Bluesbreakers featured a guitarist by the name of

Eric Clapton, talented but rather unreliable, who had decided to head over to Greece with various other musicians on a working holiday. Mayall, rather miffed, advertised for a replacement and, at a gig at the Flamingo Club in London's Wardour Street, Peter Green turned up and — rather out of character — demanded a chance to get up and play. Mayall was impressed by what he heard and offered Green the chance to take Clapton's place, at least until he returned from Greece.

What took place over the next few years was an interesting interpretation of musical chairs. When Clapton returned he reclaimed his place as the Bluesbreakers' guitarist and Peter Green moved on to join another blues band with Hammond organist Peter Bardens, called Peter B's Looners, featuring on the drum seat the lanky young Mick Fleetwood. Although Mick wasn't initially impressed by Peter Green's guitar playing (Peter Bardens told him: "You're wrong. This guy is special,") the band persevered but went nowhere fast. Bardens decided to relaunch them as Shotgun Express, a white soul band with Rod Stewart on vocals.

Peter Green wasn't so sure about it — he wanted to maintain his commitment to the blues and, so, when Clapton left John Mayall's Bluesbreakers yet again (to form Cream), he jumped back on board, and the band now featured a 17-year-old bass player called John McVie. John's friend and close neighbour was a man called Cliff Barton who played bass for Cyril Davies's R 'n' B All-Stars (Cyril had left Blues Incorporated in 1962 because he disagreed with Alexis Korner as to which way the band should progress). Cliff Barton turned down the opportunity to join the Bluesbreakers but introduced John Mayall to his friend, John McVie, who would go on to be the Bluesbreakers' bass player for more than four years (ignoring

the one or two short gaps when he would be sacked for drunken behaviour).

Similarly, Mick Fleetwood had left school in Cornwall and moved to Notting Hill in London to live with his sister and try to find work as a drummer. Just like his soon to be band mate, John McVie, Mick was lucky to discover that Peter Bardens lived just a few doors away and, having heard Mick practising drums through his open bedroom window, knocked on the door and invited him to join his then band, the Cheynes.

It was the open door Mick needed to become part of the British blues boom. Although Peter Bardens left the Cheynes in April 1965 to join Van Morrison's band, Them (and later formed the British prog rock band Camel), Mick joined another band, the Bo Street Runners for a few months, then Peter B's Looners, and finally joined John Mayall's Bluesbreakers in April 1967, replacing the great Aynsley Dunbar. For the first time, Peter, Mick and John were together. But not for long.

Mick only lasted six weeks with John Mayall's band and was sacked because of his heavy drinking. However, during that period, Mayall bought some studio time as a birthday gift for Peter Green and the three band members recorded a few songs at Decca Studios in north London, including one that Peter decided to dedicate to the rhythm section he had come to admire very much: "I've got a name for that one," said Peter. "I'm calling that tune 'Fleetwood Mac'."

Neither Peter nor John was planning to leave the Bluesbreakers (and Mick didn't want to) but something had happened during those few hours together in Decca Studios.

IN THEIR OWN MINDS, THE SEEDS OF FLEETWOOD MAC HAD BEEN SOWN.

RIGHT

John Mayall's Bluesbreakers; L-R: Mayall, Eric Clapton, John McVie and Hughie Flint. Cover shot for 1966's often called 'Beano Album'

CHAPTER 2:
MR WONDERFUL
PETER GREEN'S FLEETWOOD MAC

It wasn't long after Peter Green recorded with John McVie and Mick Fleetwood for the first time that he decided he wasn't happy anymore in the Bluesbreakers and would head over to Chicago on a fact-finding mission, dragging John McVie along with him. They were even thinking of moving out to Chicago permanently in an attempt to broaden their horizons and work with some of America's best blues musicians.

His frustration, Peter told *Record Mirror*, was that he wasn't happy with the material the Bluesbreakers were playing. He said, "It was becoming, for me, less and less of the blues. And we'd do the same thing every night. John would say something to the audience and count us in, and I'd groan inwardly."

In that frame of mind it was no surprise that both he and John McVie resigned from the Bluesbreakers at the end of May 1967 and began to plan a new band featuring the two of them and Mick Fleetwood. It would be called Fleetwood Mac. An historic moment … although, a week or so later, McVie changed his mind on the basis that regular work and a regular income from the Bluesbreakers was not something to be tossed aside lightly.

Even more frustrated, Peter Green headed off to Spain for a holiday with his girlfriend, Sandra Elsdon, to contemplate his future. He returned a few days later having made the decision to abandon the move to Chicago but press on with a new band that would play Chicago-style blues. Mick Fleetwood would be on drums; they would look for another guitarist and a new bass player; and even though John wasn't joining, they would still be called Fleetwood Mac.

From the outset, the sound engineer at Decca studios, Mike Vernon (who had taken care of Peter, John and Mick's first recordings together), had encouraged Peter Green to form his own band and was also in the process with his brother, Richard, of launching his own record company, Blue Horizon. They were looking for new bands to help launch his company, and Fleetwood Mac would be the perfect headliner.

Working with Peter not long before he decided to leave the Bluesbreakers, Mike told him about an excellent young slide guitarist he knew called Jeremy Spencer, a diminutive (just 5ft 4in tall) but very talented guitarist who was currently with a band called the Levi Set, based in Staffordshire. When the Levi Set supported the Bluesbreakers one night, Peter was very impressed, particularly with Jeremy's slide guitar skills in covering various songs by the famous American blues slide guitarist Elmore James — his obsession.

Later that evening he took him to one side to find out if he would be interested in joining his new band. Jeremy was very interested…

Over the next few weeks several top-notch bass players tried out with them, including Ric Grech (at that time a member of the Leicester-based band, Family, and who later joined the first rock supergroup, Blind Faith), and Bruce Thomas, who later joined Elvis Costello and the Attractions, but neither worked out. Peter ultimately had no choice but to place an ad in *Melody Maker* for a bass player and finally chose a young student teacher called Bob Brunning. Bob was a member of Five's Company, a house band at St Mark's & St John's College of Education in London, who had some experience of recording with Pye Records.

Fleetwood Mac, in truth, was a giant leap for Bob, but Peter had little choice because the phone number displayed in the *Melody Maker* ad was incorrect, and Bob was the only one who had contacted the newspaper to find out the correct details. As a result, Bob was offered the job on the basis that John McVie

RIGHT

Peter Green plays at a free concert in Hyde Park, London, August 1968

would take over if he changed his mind again.

Once the band line-up had been established, Mike Vernon immediately offered Fleetwood Mac a record deal, and the band's first gig was organised by Clifford Davis (a booking agent at the Rik Gunnell organization in London), who would shortly become Fleetwood Mac's manager. While most new bands might start off in some London pub, Fleetwood Mac's first gig would be at the prestigious National Jazz Pop Ballads & Blues Festival (now known as Reading Festival) held in Windsor just five weeks later.

The festival lineup would include the Small Faces, Donovan, Pentangle, the Crazy World of Arthur Brown, the Nice, Chicken Shack (featuring keyboard player Christine Perfect), Jeff Beck, Cream and … John Mayall's Bluesbreakers; in effect, it was the second British blues boom. If Fleetwood Mac wanted to be part of it, it was time for them to start rehearsing long and hard (in the Black Bull pub on London's Fulham Rd) over the next few weeks. It paid off: they went down very well on the festival's final day (Sunday 13 August 1967) in front of over 15,000 people and received some excellent press reviews.

Backstage they bumped into John McVie, who had played the night before with the Bluesbreakers. Some reports suggest he hadn't been particularly impressed by Fleetwood Mac's debut performance but, just like Peter Green, was frustrated with John Mayall's leanings towards jazzier sounds. Within a few weeks John had quit the Bluesbreakers to join Fleetwood Mac. "Instantaneous," he said. "It was a great union, great chemistry, especially with Jeremy; he was fucking brilliant."

Christine Perfect was definitely impressed by Fleetwood Mac (especially Peter Green who, she admits, she fancied very much) but she'd also enjoyed watching the Bluesbreakers, with Mr McVie on bass… Christine began to learn the piano at the age of four and was being groomed for a career in classical music until, in her early teens, she discovered the blues and rock music. As she commented: "Goodbye Schubert, hello rock 'n' roll."

Not only was Christine very talented as a musician but also as an artist, having studied sculpture at an art college in Birmingham, where

RIGHT

Peter Green, John McVie, Jeremy Spencer and Mick Fleetwood in one of their first band promo shots, 1967

she mixed with other musicians. Her first band was Shades of Blue, including Stan Webb and Andy Silvester who would go on to form the blues band Chicken Shack.

After such an excellent response at their debut gig, Fleetwood Mac began working flat out across the UK, immediately attracting a huge fan base of appreciative blues enthusiasts. John McVie's decision to join Fleetwood Mac had been bad luck for Bob Brunning, but before John arrived he did at least become part of rock history by recording several songs with the band at Decca Studios, thanks to sound engineer Mike Vernon who smuggled them in at night to use the facilities free of charge.

Fleetwood Mac's first single, 'I Believe My Time Ain't Long', released in November 1967, featured 'Rambling Pony' on the B-side (with Bob Brunning on bass) and was released on CBS Records when Decca turned it down. Their second single, 'Black Magic Woman', released March 1968, featured 'The Sun is Shining' on the B-side in the UK, or 'Long Grey Mare' (with Bob Brunning once again on bass) for the US market.

Their first LP, the eponymous *Fleetwood Mac* (often referred to as the 'Dog and Dustbin' album due to the cover photograph) was recorded at CBS Studios in New Bond Street in London and released in February 1968. It was very well received by the press and public alike, reaching No. 4 in the UK charts. Said *Melody Maker*: "This is the best English blues LP ever released."

Within eight months of their first rehearsal together, Fleetwood Mac shot from nowhere to becoming what Mike Vernon described as "the biggest draw around". The band began to play at least 10 gigs a month across the UK, with queues around the block to see them.

With such a level of success there was pressure on the band to produce their second LP, *Mr Wonderful*, released in August 1968. The result was an album that had been rushed out too soon and was recorded virtually as a live performance in the studio, which proved not so popular with some members of the press. "Rather dull," commented *Melody Maker*, while slightly disappointing sales meant the LP only reached No. 10 in the UK.

It wasn't a disaster and there were some positives to enjoy, the most important being the first performance on a Fleetwood Mac LP by Christine Perfect (by this time John McVie's girlfriend), whose keyboard skills added new depth to the band's overall sound. In August '68, she and John McVie were married; two weeks later, Jeremy Spencer married his childhood sweetheart, Fiona.

Surprisingly, however, given that it was one of the reasons why Peter Green had wanted to leave the Bluesbreakers in the first place, it was clear that he now wanted to extend the band's sound away from just pure blues to something broader and more experimental. Between their first two LPs, the band paid a brief visit to the USA in June '68 for a handful of performances, where they met and mingled with the likes of the Grateful Dead, and Janis Joplin's Big Brother & the Holding Company.

As good as Jeremy Spencer's slide guitar skills were, Peter had become a little jaded by his reluctance to progress musically, rather than remain obsessed with Elmore James parodies. Although his performances were often hilariously entertaining, he was also prone to vulgar stage antics such as performing with beer-filled condoms and a giant dildo — the likes of which had resulted in Fleetwood Mac being banned from the London Marquee for a while.

Peter was aware of another talented 17-year-old guitarist called Danny Kirwan from Brixton in south London, whose band called Boilerhouse had supported Fleetwood Mac several times from 1967-68. He and Mike Vernon were hugely impressed by Danny's unique guitar technique and were keen to sign him to Blue Horizon, but felt that the other members of the band weren't good enough. They'd done their best to find replacement musicians of higher quality, but failed miserably. In typical fashion, Mick Fleetwood simply said, "Why don't we just ask him to join the Mac?"

Danny Kirwan's individual, harmonic guitar sound (influenced by the Shadows' Hank Marvin and French jazz guitarist, Django Reinhardt), plus his skills as a vocalist and songwriter, would affect the whole band and help them discover the new sort of sound Green had been searching for. As Mick Fleetwood commented: "We were about to mutate into another kind of band altogether."

RIGHT
_____

More dustbins! Chicken Shack L-R: Andy Silvester, Christine Perfect, Dave Bidwell, Stan Webb. Blue Horizon promo, 1968

The band's third single, the beautiful slow ballad, 'Need Your Love So Bad', coupled with B-side 'Stop Messin' Round', was released on 5 July 1968 and proved to be the last pure blues song the band would record as Fleetwood Mac. (However, in January 1969 they did contribute to the jam sessions at the famous Chess Ter-Mar Studios in Chicago with the likes of Otis Spann, Willie Dixon and Buddy Guy.)

Two months after joining them, Kirwan contributed 'Jigsaw Puzzle Blues', a Django Reinhardt-inspired song that was the perfect B-side for Green's greatest ever instrumental. Flying back over the Atlantic from their first USA visit, while staring out of the window, a three-note guitar intro emerged from Peter's head. He noted it down and later decided to use it as the basis of a song, with the help of Danny's unique ambient sound. The song was called 'Albatross', inspired (according to Christine McVie), by the pastoral music of the English composer, Vaughan Williams. A beautiful musical seascape, it was totally different to anything Fleetwood Mac had previously recorded, and was viewed rather suspiciously by the British media. Radio One DJ John Peel hated it, while *Disc* magazine said: "Excellent — but hardly chart material."

At the beginning of December '68 the band set off to New York to begin their first proper US tour over more than two months. It meant the band would not be in the UK to promote 'Albatross', but it soon became clear they really didn't need to. Its constant playing on the radio and TV did the job for them. The public loved 'Albatross' so much that it slowly climbed the charts over the next few weeks and reached No. 1 in the UK by February '69.

Towards the end of the successful US tour they went into a New York studio and recorded their next single, the equally moving 'Man of the World' concerning a man who has everything except the thing he wants most — a relationship. Coupled with a Jeremy Spencer rockabilly parody, 'Somebody's Gonna Get Their Head Kicked in Tonite', it made it to No. 2 in the UK charts. Jeremy hadn't contributed to 'Albatross' or 'Man of the World' at all and, when the band returned from America and prepared to record their third studio LP, he made it clear he didn't want anything to do with that either. He preferred to concentrate on

his own solo album, so they just let him get on with it.

Unbelievably, the single 'Man of the World' was not released by Blue Horizon because Fleetwood Mac's contract had expired. Fleetwood Mac had been signed to a one-year recording deal with a two-year option to renew it if the Vernons wished to do so, which, of course, they did. But they had been so busy arranging a substantial deal with CBS Records that they forgot all about the renewal date, and now it was too late.

Clifford Davis began to hammer out a new deal with CBS's rivals, Warner Bros, and, in order to release another single as quickly as possible for use as negotiating ammunition, arranged for 'Man of the World' to be recorded in New York and released by Immediate Records, an independent British label launched in 1965 by the Rolling Stones' manager, Andrew Loog Oldham and which, until recently, had been linked to CBS. There was hope that a long-term deal could be brokered with Immediate but, once the single was released, financial problems immediately surfaced and Immediate ceased operation in 1970.

Clifford returned to Warner Bros and a new deal was signed for Fleetwood Mac to record with their offshoot label, Reprise Records, founded by Frank Sinatra in 1960. The band remains with them to this day. Peter Green had been seriously upset by the way Mike and Richard Vernon had been treated when their Blue Horizon record deal was not renewed and made it clear in an interview with *New Musical Express* that he did not want to be part of what he called the "cut and dried" music business.

The good news for their new LP released on Reprise was that the four contributing members of the band, with help from Christine McVie on keyboards, now had plenty of time to write and record it. The result, *Then Play On*, was by far the best of the three Peter Green LPs, inspired by the Beatles, American acid rock, British folk, and jazzy easy listening far more than pure blues. They also recorded yet another hit single, the stunning 'Oh Well (Parts 1 and 2)', which made it to No. 2 in the UK and No. 55 in the USA — their first American single to chart. Initially a throbbing hard rocker, it begins with superb guitar from Peter Green followed by his opening vocal:

LEFT
_____

Los Angeles, 1969: (L-R) John McVie, Danny Kirwan, Mick Fleetwood, Peter Green and Jeremy Spencer

'I can't help it 'bout the shape I'm in,
I can't sing, I ain't pretty, and my legs are thin,
But don't ask me what I think of you,
I might not give the answer that you want me to.
Oh well.'

Just one more verse and chorus and the song transposes into a beautiful, concerto-like, classical guitar piece. In truth, this was virtually a solo single from Peter. For the concerto he played all of the instruments himself except recorder parts provided by his girlfriend, Sandra, and some additional background piano fills played by Jeremy Spencer.

Peter's lyrics, however, were further suggesting he was far from happy with his life. The single, 'Man of the World' contained the line: 'There's no one I'd rather be but I just wish that I'd never been born.' His final Fleetwood Mac single was the equally brilliant but even more disturbing 'The Green Manalishi (with the Two Prong Crown)', released in May 1970. Peter explained that he had written the song based on a nightmare about a vicious green dog that represented the power of the devil and money.

Despite his devout religious beliefs, musical genius and huge critical success, it became clear Peter was fighting a descent into madness. His Jewish faith was renounced, he gave away significant amounts of money to various charities and asked the other band members to do the same (which they refused), and had experimented with LSD and other drugs while on tour in America, influenced by members of the Grateful Dead and other musicians.

The final crisis is reported to have taken place in Munich, Germany, on 22 March 1970 when Peter and one of their roadies, Dennis Keane, attended a party with a group of hippies known as the Munich Jet Set, who gave them some very potent LSD. A bad trip had a major impact on his mental health and he had to be rescued by Clifford Davis, Mick Fleetwood and some of the road crew the following day. Some say he was never the same again.

In later years Peter claimed the incident had been exaggerated and what the 'bad trip' had actually done was help him think clearly and realise he no longer wanted to be in Fleetwood Mac.

Two days later the band headed off to Germany and then Scandinavia for a short run of concerts. The performances went well but, while travelling through Sweden on the tour bus at the beginning of April, Peter sat down next to Clifford Davis and told him he was leaving the band. There were various reasons: he wanted to play with other musicians who wouldn't constrain him; he was frustrated with Mick Fleetwood's rhythmic timing; even more frustrated with John's McVie's drinking; he didn't like Danny Kirwan at all; the only member of the band he got on well with was Jeremy Spencer — quite likely because he was hardly ever in the studio! He did, however, say that he would not let the band down and honour any existing commitments.

In an interview with Nick Logan in *New Musical Express* he said: "I feel it is time to change. I am always concerned with what is right with God and what God would have me do … whatever I do — whether I form another group or not — I need to be with people who feel exactly the same as I do … [the other band members] were disturbed when I told them and shook up a bit."

An understatement. Peter's final performance with Fleetwood Mac was at a poorly attended one-day festival held at Bath City's football ground on Saturday 23 May 1970. It was a sad and inappropriate way to say goodbye.

Said John McVie: "It was very hard to find yourself out on a limb without Peter who had become the band's writer, guitar hero, lead singer and the main focal point of the band. And for that to go, I mean, it was very traumatic."

Mick Fleetwood summed things up rather more melodramatically: "Losing Peter was like taking the rudder out of a sailing boat. As a band we were still afloat, but we were drifting with no map and no land in sight."

MR WONDERFUL HAD SAILED AWAY.

RIGHT

Peter Green wearing white monk's robes while performing on a TV show, London, England, 1969

CHAPTER 3:
BARE TREES
FLEETWOOD MAC'S WILDERNESS YEARS, PART 1

BEING LEFT AFLOAT, AS MICK DESCRIBED IT, WITHOUT A RUDDER, IT WAS NO GREAT SURPRISE THAT THINGS STARTED TO GET A LITTLE BIT CHOPPY FOR FLEETWOOD MAC.

Before Peter Green had even left the band it was decided that, in an attempt to steady the ship, they needed to get away from the distractions of London and find an environment where they could all work and live together, with their families and the road crew, in harmony. Little chance of that. For a start, Peter wanted nothing to do with it and continued to live at home with his parents in Surrey.

Clifford Davis found the others a perfect, very remote six-bedroomed house to lease in Hampshire, called Kiln House. Early in March 1970 they loaded up their belongings and moved in together like a family of musical Beverley Hillbillies who had just struck oil. It wasn't long, of course, before more cracks, began to appear.

With Peter gone it was up to Jeremy and Danny to start filling some of those musical cracks at least, but it was clear from the outset that they wouldn't find it easy. There were signs of stress almost immediately and both began to behave at times rather strangely. Jeremy, a devout Christian, spent much of his time in his bedroom studying the Bible with his wife, Fiona, while Danny, having to shoulder the burden of a volatile relationship with his unstable girlfriend, Claire, started to drink increasingly heavily and would be prone to angry outbursts for no apparent reason.

A more positive event at Kiln House was when Mick tied the knot with his girlfriend, Jenny Boyd — the sister of Patti Boyd who at that time was married to Beatle, George Harrison, and later Eric Clapton. The song 'Jennifer Juniper' by Donavan was written about Jenny. The wedding took place on 20 June and

Peter Green did attend, but turned up too late to fulfill his role as Mick's best man. John McVie wasn't keen, so the roadcrew member, Dennis Keane, took responsibility for that honour. Their first daughter Amelia (or Amy) was born in January 1971.

Christine McVie had left Chicken Shack in August 1969 to launch her solo career on Blue Horizon Records. Despite winning, for two years running, the *Melody Maker* 'Female Vocalist of the Year' award, and her LP, *Christine Perfect*, being critically well-received, going solo had not proved a financial success. Living in Kiln House with John, she'd spent most of her time adding keyboards to Fleetwood Mac's rehearsals as they prepared to head over to the USA to promote their first LP minus Peter Green. Without him, the sound was too thin, and Christine's contributions solved the problem perfectly. When they left for America on 1 August, she went with them. Within a week, Mick Fleetwood asked her to join the band.

The new LP, called *Kiln House*, to celebrate their communal living, was released on 18 September 1970 and, despite being very different to *Then Play On*, was reasonably well-received. 'Forwards in terms of production and backwards in their search for material and style,' said Chris Welch in *Melody Maker*, but, despite the overload of Jeremy Spencer's rock 'n' roll parodies, it did contain four excellent new songs from Danny Kirwan. Overall, very promising.

In early 1971 the band were due to head back to the USA for another promotional tour, during which time the lease on Kiln House would expire. It was decided that it would be more sensible to combine their funds and purchase suitable alternative accommodation. Mick Fleetwood found the perfect place just a few miles from Kiln House. Benifold was a large, 22-roomed, Victorian mansion, which Clifford purchased for the band for

RIGHT

L-R: Christine McVie, John McVie, Mick Fleetwood, Jeremy Spencer's replacement, Bob Welch, and Danny Kirwan

£23,000. It would become their home, rehearsal room and sometimes a recording studio for the next three and a half years.

The 1971 tour began at the Fillmore West in San Francisco for four nights before heading off to Los Angeles; the night before they were leaving, however, the San Fernando earthquake took place, killing over 60 people and causing huge damage to buildings over a wide area. Understandably the band were concerned about flying into LA — especially Jeremy Spencer who felt something 'evil' was taking place — but were reassured that they would not be in any danger and their concert at the famous Whisky A Go Go club that night would go ahead.

When they arrived in LA that morning, Jeremy seemed to have calmed down and, soon after checking into the hotel, went out to visit one of his favourite bookshops on Hollywood Boulevard. By 6pm, with the band due to set off to the gig, there was no sign of Jeremy. Tour manager, Phil McDonnell, and roadie, Dennis Keane, went out to look for him, but to no avail. Very concerned, the band cancelled the show, contacted the police, put out a radio appeal and organised a search party. Phil and Dennis trawled the Hollywood and Sunset Boulevard area with Jeremy's picture, stopping people in the street and asking if they'd seen him. This went on for four days until they were tipped off by a member of a religious group that Jeremy was with another cult, the Children of God — an organisation accused several times of encouraging sexual assault of women and children.

Clifford, Phil McDonnell and Dennis Keane went to the cult's headquarters in downtown LA to confront Jeremy in an effort to persuade him to come back to the hotel, but he adamantly refused. Jeremy had always been quite particular about his clothes and appearance but was wearing an old white shirt several sizes too big for him, white trousers, a pair of flip flops and his hair had been cut short, but he appeared calm — happy, in fact. Whatever they said to him, his response was, "Jesus loves you." Despite claims that he had been brainwashed and forced to join the organisation, Jeremy wanted nothing more to do with Fleetwood Mac and could not be persuaded to change his mind.

Spencer and his wife Fiona moved to America and have been members (now called the Family International) ever since. They eventually had four more children together in addition to their son, Dicon, but separated in 1978 and are now divorced. Jeremy has continued to play music and formed various bands within the organisation, living around the world and playing primarily at religious festivals to promote their work and beliefs. He has also recorded several albums, but with little commercial success.

There were six weeks of the tour remaining and Clifford faced the reality that, if they cancelled it, they could lose so much money that they would lose the beloved new Benifold mansion. He could see no option other than to ring Peter Green back in the UK and plead with him to come over and save their souls. At that stage Peter had virtually given up music and was working on a farm, but amazingly he agreed to come over to bail out his former colleagues.

Although he knew little of the new material, he agreed to play some of the older hits such as 'Black Magic Woman', but would then set off on long blues jams in the style of the Allman Brothers Band. He loved the Allman Brothers and had even got up and played with them towards the end of 1970 in New Orleans, and was hugely impressed by Duane Allman and Dickey Betts's extended blues instrumentals. Not surprisingly, the audiences loved them as well and the remainder of Fleetwood Mac's potentially disastrous tour proved a great success.

The band returned to Benifold exhausted, but there was little time to rest. First, a new single was released in March — 'Dragonfly', written by Danny, with 'The Purple Dancer' on the B-side composed by Danny, Mick and John. It was a nice 'Albatross'-style ballad, but failed to make it to the charts either in the UK or USA.

More importantly, with Jeremy now living with the Children of God, they needed a replacement guitarist as quickly as possible. One of the band's close acquaintances — a Californian called Judy Wong, who was married to Jethro Tull's bass player, Glenn Cornick — was friends with an LA native called Bob Welch, who she knew was currently living in Paris and looking for work. She contacted him and arranged an audition.

Although he'd hit hard times, Bob was a seasoned professional who had played with the likes of James Brown and Aretha Franklin. The band loved his sound and, as a bonus, he was also a prolific songwriter. He played them a few examples and they liked what they heard. He stayed at Benifold for a couple of weeks so they could judge whether or not he'd fit the bill — even attending Danny Kirwan's marriage to Claire during that period. Finally, in April '71, he was offered the job.

After a few weeks of rehearsals at Benifold, it was then back on the road to various smaller UK venues to try out new material, including some of Bob's own songs, before heading over to Advision Studios in London to record a new LP, *Future Games*, released in September 1971. With two songs from Christine, two from Bob Welch, three from Danny Kirwan and one accredited to the whole band, the album combines a real mishmash of styles, which didn't meet with approval from either the press or public — only just making it to No. 91 in the US charts and nowhere in the UK.

Some fans feel *Future Games* is one of Fleetwood Mac's best albums and much underappreciated, even today. Just six months later, despite being on tour across the USA and Europe virtually flat out, the band released another LP, *Bare Trees*, which, although not quite as good, continued in the same vein as *Future Games*: laid back '70s sounds, great songs and wonderful twin guitar work and vocal harmonies from Danny and Bob. The combination of a south London lad with a Hollywood hippie shouldn't really have worked at all … but it worked brilliantly. Musically, at least.

Personally, however, more Fleetwood Mac turmoil was just below the surface. The band had been working incredibly hard for over a year, either touring together or living together at Benifold. The married couples had all been under a lot of stress, particularly John and Christine, and Bob was finding it increasingly difficult to work with Danny, who was showing signs of paranoia, convinced nobody liked his songs, or his guitar playing or anything much else about him. As a result, he and Bob would fall out on a regular basis and often have to be pulled apart.

A time bomb was waiting to explode and it stopped ticking just before the band went on stage somewhere in New York State in America. Bob and Danny were tuning their guitars but couldn't agree whose instrument was out of tune. It developed into an argument, then a fight, and Danny exploded. Screaming incoherently, he beat his head and fists against a wall before, bleeding quite badly, picked up his lovely Gibson Les Paul guitar and smashed it to smithereens, then stormed out of the changing room and refused to go on stage.

The band, open-mouthed in shock, had no option but to perform without him, apologising for his absence by claiming he had been taken ill, which he certainly had. Unknown to the band he sat at the sound desk with tour manager and sound engineer, Phil McDonnell, watching them flounder through a buttock-clenching performance and then had the nerve, after the show, to criticise them for making too many mistakes.

The band had had enough and demanded that Danny be fired there and then. Mick was a little more cautious because he knew that sacking Danny would mean the rest of the tour being cancelled. With Clifford Davis back in the UK, it was Mick's decision. The next day he went to Danny's room and told him the band were agreed that he should leave. Phil McDonnell was given the job of driving Danny to JFK airport for a flight back to the UK. The band followed soon after and the press were informed that Danny had left because he wanted to concentrate on his own solo material; in reality, he'd been fired.

Yet again there was a desperate need to find another guitarist quickly. Mick had been impressed by an English slide guitarist from Plymouth called Bob Weston. Currently with Long John Baldry, whose band had supported Fleetwood Mac during the '71 UK tour, he had an impeccable musical background having previously performed with the blues godfathers Alexis Korner and Cyril Davies.

Someone — probably Clifford Davis — had also made the decision that the band needed a new, more dynamic front man to handle vocals, and was aware that the singer for British blues band Savoy Brown, Dave Walker, was looking to make a move.

Both he and Bob Weston were approached in the autumn of 1972 and both happily accepted new roles with Fleetwood Mac.

Six weeks of rehearsals took place at Benifold before heading off on a Scandinavian tour, which all went well. In January 1973, work began on a new album at Benifold, using the Rolling Stones' mobile recording unit. Released two months later, *Penguin* wasn't a disaster, but it certainly wasn't great, either. The most obvious questions were why Dave Walker had contributed so little to the LP and, even more intriguing, why he had been invited to join the band in the first place? Certainly the other members of the band were asking the same question.

There were more questions about the next album, *Mystery to Me*, recorded just a few months later at Benifold. To begin with, Mick, John and Christine had decided there was no role for Dave Walker in Fleetwood Mac and asked Clifford to sack him. The feeling was that when *Penguin* was recorded, he had spent most of his time in a nearby pub (often with John McVie), but that was largely because he had nothing else to do. Additionally they felt that on stage he was tending to hog the limelight as a front vocalist, which was not the way to carry on in Fleetwood Mac. Reluctantly, in June 1973, Clifford told Dave Walker they were letting him go.

Recording for *Mystery to Me* got underway properly as soon as Dave Walker had gone, but it was soon clear that there were more serious issues to deal with than just someone hogging the limelight. John and Christine's marriage was on the rocks and it was obvious to everyone that Christine was having an affair with their recording engineer, Martin Birch. In response, John was playing the field and drinking even more. The tension in the recording studio, at times, was unbearable.

Mystery to Me was released in October '73 to a very mixed reception from the press, despite the fact that it contained some great songs; of the 12, all but one were written by Bob Welch or Christine McVie, individually or together. But the record, and the band, lacked any real focus. For example, the one remaining track on the LP was a cover version of the Yardbirds' hit 'For Your Love', and that was the song they released as a single! The B-side, 'Hypnotized' by Bob Welch, was one of the best tracks

LEFT

Image from 1972's *Penguin* cover shoot: (L-R) Christine McVie, Dave Walker, Bob Welch, Mick Fleetwood, Bob Weston, John McVie

on the LP and was the song that got played repeatedly on radio stations across America — perfectly indicating the direction in which Fleetwood Mac were heading, but the band didn't seem to understand that themselves. 'For Your Love' was Fleetwood Mac's ninth consecutive single not to chart in either America or the UK.

A month or so before *Mystery to Me* was released the band set off to America once again to promote the album. Within a couple of weeks, Jenny admitted to Mick Fleetwood that she was having an affair with Bob Weston. Jenny had come on the tour with their two daughters, Amelia and Lucy, and it was soon clear that Bob was spending a lot more time with them than their father. Mick was totally focused on the band and the music business and didn't seem to recognise the fact that he wasn't paying his own family enough attention.

Once Mick knew what was going on, Jenny left the tour with their two girls and flew to Los Angeles to stay with Bob Welch's girlfriend, Nancy, for a few days, then headed back to England to stay at the Faces' Ronnie Wood and his wife Krissy's house in Richmond.

Being true pros the tour continued for a few more shows but was proving increasingly difficult for everyone, especially Mick. After the shows he would sit with tour manager Phil McDonnell until the early hours of the morning pouring his heart out; both of them barely slept for five nights and Mick wasn't eating properly either. He was on the verge of a nervous breakdown.

In Lincoln, Nebraska, on 20 October 1973, Mick broke down in tears and decided he couldn't take it anymore. Bob Weston was sacked and handed a plane ticket by Phil McDonnell, then delivered to the airport. The remaining 26 dates of the tour were cancelled and the other band members abandoned ship, eventually heading off in four different directions to get as far away from each other as possible: Mick initially back to the UK (before heading off to Zambia), John to Hawaii (before heading to Los Angeles), Bob Welch to Los Angeles, while Christine stayed with Phil McDonnell in New York for a few days while he dealt with the fallout caused by so many cancellations, then returned with him back to Benifold.

Clifford Davis sat in England totally devastated, trying to calculate the financial damage caused and how to deal with this latest melodramatic episode in...

...FLEETWOOD MAC'S ROCK 'N' ROLL SOAP OPERA.

RIGHT

Tension palpable in this 1973 promo shot: (clockwise) Christine McVie, Mick Fleetwood, Bob Weston, Bob Welch, John McVie

CHAPTER 4:

HEROES ARE HARD TO FIND

WILL THE REAL FLEETWOOD MAC PLEASE STAND UP

THERE ARE TIMES WHEN IT'S HARD TO BELIEVE SOME OF THE MANY CURIOUS INCIDENTS THAT TOOK PLACE DURING FLEETWOOD MAC'S LONG AND VOLATILE CONTRIBUTION TO ROCK HISTORY, BUT THIS IS THE MOST BIZARRE OF THEM ALL.

Fleetwood Mac's manager, Clifford Davis, staring financial ruin in the face due to the 1973 US tour being cancelled, had reached the conclusion that the real Fleetwood Mac's days were over for Bob Welch, Mick Fleetwood and the McVies. What happened next is all highly debatable. Clifford says he took part in a teleconference with the band members and tour manager Phil McDonnell to inform him that the tour was cancelled and the band were splitting up. When they returned to the UK, Mick Fleetwood and Christine McVie went to Clifford's house in Woldingham, Surrey, on 10 November 1973 to discuss the situation and see what, if anything, could be done.

Christine told him that she was in love with Martin Birch and would be recording a solo LP with him, and asked Clifford if he would finance it; he agreed. She said she no longer wanted to be part of Fleetwood Mac. Clifford Davis was told that John McVie had also decided to leave the band because of his marital problems with Christine.

It has been suggested that Clifford believed he owned the rights to the name Fleetwood Mac and suggested to Mick Fleetwood that he could form a new version of the band under that name. Other sources have said it was Mick's idea to put a new band together because he was desperate to carry on; without a band, he felt he was left with nothing. Clifford wasn't

so sure it was a good idea and turned for advice to Fleetwood Mac's ATI (American Talent International) booking agent, Bruce Payne (later Deep Purple's manager), who suggested there was no reason why Mick couldn't form a new Fleetwood Mac — the band was named after him, after all!

On that basis, Clifford contacted musicians from other bands he was involved with who he thought would be ideal: Kirby Gregory (previously with Curved Air) on guitar and Elmer Gantry (real name Dave Terry, from Velvet Opera) on guitar and vocals. Phil McDonnell was put in charge of holding auditions to find suitable session musicians to fill the other vacancies, which resulted in Paul Martinez on bass and John Wilkinson on keyboards. Phil also set up rehearsals for the new Fleetwood Mac in the middle of December 1973.

Two weeks before the tour was due to start, Mick contacted Clifford and told him to cancel the first two weeks because he needed more time with Jenny to try to sort out their marital problems. Clifford refused, saying understandably that after what had already happened, it would prove to be a disaster. Instead he agreed to get another musician to handle the first few gigs — a session drummer called Craig Collinge — until Mick was well enough to join the tour.

A few days before he was due to fly over to the States, Phil McDonnell met up with John and Mick at the Chelsea Potter pub in London's King's Road to discuss what was going to happen. When Mick went across the road to visit his tailor's shop in the King's Road, where he bought his bespoke suits, John asked Phil if Mick really intended to be part of the new band; Phil

RIGHT

John McVie, Mick Fleetwood, Bob Welch and Christine McVie under the Hollywood Sign soon after relocating to LA in 1974

confirmed that was the case. When he got a chance to speak to Mick on his own, Phil checked that he really did intend to join the US tour. Mick said he definitely would be. The night before he set off to the US with the new Fleetwood Mac, Phil saw Mick in the Speakeasy club in London and he seemed to be looking forward to joining the tour in a few days time. Mick even checked that Craig Collinge definitely knew the drum seat was only on a temporary basis. Phil assured him that Craig was well-aware. Phil also spoke to Christine that night, who wished them well. Nobody seemed to have any problems with the situation at all.

But now, for another side of the story. Bob Welch was in Los Angeles and claimed that in December he saw a newspaper story (or possibly a poster) promoting the new Fleetwood Mac gigs, featuring Mick Fleetwood and … what!? … Christine McVie. It was also claimed that Clifford Davis had informed the trade press that John and Bob had left the band. Bob Welch contacted the other band members and suggested he should come over to England. He said they should seize this opportunity to make use of the publicity created by the 'fake' Fleetwood Mac and contact the media.

In an interview with *Rolling Stone* magazine, before he left California, Bob said: "It is a rip-off. The manager put together a group real fast using the name Fleetwood Mac before we had a chance to do anything about it. We all got letters from Clifford Davis indicating his intentions to put a new band back on the road. He issued an ultimatum to all of us. In effect, what happened was that we got offered gigs, which is not really his place to do. We said, 'Well, hell, we're not going to do that. We want to go back on the road in such-and-such length of time.' Nobody accepted the offer, and so the guy proceeded to get together another band, and he worked with ATI [American Talent International], the agency, and they went out to grab the big bucks. He can put four dogs barking on a leash and call it Fleetwood Mac. Basically what it boils down to is the manager flipped his lid. We're going to take legal action as soon as we know where we can take it from."

Rolling Stone also spoke to Fleetwood Mac's booking agent, Bruce Payne, who denied Welch's version of events and said the problem had been caused by the original band's 'bitterness'.

HE BACKED UP CLIFFORD'S VERSION OF WHAT HAD TAKEN PLACE.

As far as Phil McDonnell was aware, Mick would be arriving in Baltimore to reclaim his drum seat from Craig Collinge and stay with them for the rest of the tour. But then, sitting in his Baltimore hotel room, Phil McDonnell received a call from Mick Fleetwood to tell him he wasn't coming at all. He told Phil to come back to Benifold immediately because they wanted him to take over as their manager. Mick told him the band considered him the only person they could trust.

Phil was amazed and refused to leave the 'fake' Fleetwood Mac in the lurch. Admirably, his view was that it would be unprofessional and unfair to the musicians to do something like that. Mick handed the phone to John McVie who also asked Phil to come back, but again he refused. Instead, Phil hung up and called Clifford. Stunned, Clifford called Mick to find out what the hell was going on, but Mick refused to speak to him. Within the hour, Clifford received a call from his lawyer to be informed that Mick, Bob, John and Christine had sued him… At a later date, one can only assume acting in accordance with legal advice, all of the genuine members of Fleetwood Mac denied any knowledge of the new band or the rescheduled US tour.

But the band played on. Or, at least, the 'fake' band did. The four-month tour continued and some shows went quite well — they were good musicians who knew the songs inside out — but more and more audiences were asking questions about where Mick was, and who were these people on stage? Messages went out across US TV and radio stations that fans should not go to the shows because the musicians were imposters and the real Fleetwood Mac were being ripped off by their manager. More and more gigs were cancelled until, eventually, and not surprisingly, the rest of the tour was called off.

The 'fake' Fleetwood Mac musicians returned to England with their tails between their legs, but went on to form another real band called Stretch and had a Top 20 hit in November 1975 with the song 'Why Did You Do It?' The lyric includes the lines:

'I've been thinking 'bout what you have done to me
The damage is much deeper than you'll ever see
Hit me like a hammer to my head
I wonder were you pushed or were you led?
Why did you do it? Why did you do that thing to me?
The only one who knows the truth,
Man, it's him, me and you.

The song was aimed directly at Mick Fleetwood for not turning up in Baltimore and denying any knowledge of the new Fleetwood Mac's existence. To make it worse, it was a much better single than most of the real Fleetwood Mac's 45s over the last five years.

Mick hired the American lawyer Mickey Shapiro to represent them in the legal case, which took over four years to resolve, in as much as it ever was. By that time, the real Fleetwood Mac were hugely successful, and wealthy, so its importance had dwindled, for them at least. Clifford certainly didn't benefit and was badly affected both financially and emotionally by the whole sorry episode; so was Phil McDonnell, who never worked for the band again; John Courage, who had also been one of the crew members on the 'fake' tour, took Phil's place as tour manager. The case was eventually settled out of court.

In April 2017 Stretch's front men, Elmer Gantry and Kirby Gregory, appeared on Johnnie Walker's BBC Radio 2 show, 'Sounds of the 70s', and were interviewed about the 'fake' Fleetwood Mac debacle. This should, hopefully, put the whole rather sordid episode finally to bed. Said Elmer Gantry: "Mick Fleetwood came to our house and we talked through the new band and it all seemed fine, and Mick said, 'Well I can't actually come and rehearse with you [because it was fairly imminent going back to America to tour] but if you get in a drummer I'll join you for the tour' … and in the event we turned up in the States and Mick didn't turn up".

"We heard stories about 'we have no idea who these people are pretending to be us' and it wasn't until about three years ago that somebody sent me, anonymously, some court papers where, in court in the '70s, Mick admitted that he'd been to our house and discussed Fleetwood Mac … in Wikipedia they now have another version that's not been contested because

it's absolutely true and it's in court papers."

CERTAINLY IT HAD NOT BEEN FLEETWOOD MAC'S FINEST HOUR.

During the four-year court proceedings, Bob Welch had liaised with the other band members from Los Angeles and, by early '74, was finding his situation increasingly difficult. He suggested it would make more sense if the whole band moved over to LA where they would have better access to their legal representatives and to Warner Bros, who had been expressing concerns as to who owned the name 'Fleetwood Mac'. Eventually an agreement was reached with Warner Bros that they would continue to support Fleetwood Mac but only on the basis that, if Clifford Davis did win the case, they would be indemnified against any damages he might bring against them.

It was not an entirely satisfactory situation for the band but it did mean they could go back into the studio — Angel City Sound in LA — and record a new LP, *Heroes Are Hard to Find*. This was very much Bob Welch's record, with seven of the 11 tracks written by him, plus solid support from Christine McVie, who wrote the other four; the result is Fleetwood Mac's most diverse LP since *Then Play On*, covering a range of genres from country to jazz and West Coast soft rock to R'n'B. It's a decent LP that made it to No. 34 in the US charts but now tends to be overlooked because of what was to follow.

The band set out in September 1974 to promote *Heroes Are Hard to Find* to an appreciative audience, no doubt relieved that they actually recognised some of the musicians on stage. The tour continued successfully for the best part of four months and everything seemed to be back on track, but then, in December '74, Bob Welch informed the band that he was resigning. Everything had just piled up on top on him — the legal battle, the marital problems within the band (including his own marriage to Nancy), the incessant changes to the band's line-up, the pressure on him to contribute the majority of songs, months on the road with Mick, John and Christine and the ubiquitous 'musical differences' — all added up to the realisation that he had had enough. Said Bob, 'I had come to

the point where I didn't feel I had anything else to offer the band... Faced with the prospect of making another Fleetwood Mac record, I wouldn't have known what to do."

For once, however, the departure was dignified, with little animosity. Mick, John and Christine were initially upset when he told them he was leaving, but all recognised his importance and contribution to the band. Said Mick in his autobiography, *Play On*: "I was surprised Bob wanted to leave the fold, because he'd invested so much. After all, he lobbied us to move to America and he'd been there with me every step of the way through the tedious legal battle for our name. He didn't have to go those extra miles, but he did… We could do nothing but respect Bob and honour his decision."

All the more surprising, then, that when Fleetwood Mac were inducted into the Rock & Roll Hall of Fame in 1998, Bob Welch was not included; all of the other main band members, including Peter Green, Danny Kirwan and Jeremy Spencer, were.

A couple of weeks before Bob Welch resigned, Mick had been taking care of some chores and had driven from his home in Laurel Canyon to a grocery store to stock up on food and drink. He bumped into someone he knew vaguely from the music business, who was doing some PR work for a new recording studio in LA — Sound City — and invited Mick to come along and take a look. As it happened, Mick had been considering where they should record their next LP so threw his groceries into the boot of the car, and off they went.

Such is the way of life that the most mundane activities can change your existence forever. The story of what happened next has been recounted in various ways depending on who tells it, but it seems to be something like this:

At Sound City, Mick was very impressed by the studio layout and got on well with the house sound engineer, Keith Olsen. Sensing his interest, Keith suggested he play Mick an album he'd recorded the previous year, to demonstrate how good the sound facilities were. On their way into the control room, Mick spotted an attractive young woman laying down some vocal overdubs in one of the studio rooms.

"Who's that?" he asked. "That's Stevie Nicks," said Keith. "She's on the tape I'm going to play you."

RIGHT

Stevie Nicks at work in a recording studio, circa 1975

Keith put on the song 'Frozen Love' from an LP *Buckingham Nicks*, recorded at Sound City in 1973 — the best track on what is a very good album. While they were playing the song, a guy walked into the control room and saw Mick and Keith listening to his LP. It was Lindsey Buckingham. According to Lindsey, he didn't recognise Mick but they were briefly introduced and shook hands. When the tape finished, Mick told Keith he was really impressed, especially with the guitar player, but that was about it.

Two weeks later, Bob announced he was resigning. Once the dust had settled and Mick had had enough time to think about finding a replacement guitarist, he immediately thought of Lindsey Buckingham and rang Keith Olsen to find out if he was available. Keith explained that Lindsey was looking for work but only alongside Stevie Nicks: they were a package, a duo, said Olsen, that couldn't be separated.

Olsen was the only one who knew that Lindsey and Stevie were virtually destitute and desperate for money. *Buckingham Nicks* had been released by Polydor Records but the company had not promoted it with any real belief and sales were so poor that Lindsey and Stevie were dropped by the label very quickly. Things had got so bad that Stevie had taken day-jobs as a cleaner and a waitress to earn at least enough money to allow them to eat. When she heard Fleetwood Mac were interested in her and Lindsey joining the band, she screamed in delight! Earning some decent money meant more to her than anything. Lindsey wasn't so sure if it was the right thing to do in terms of their careers and the kind of music they wanted to make.

Mick got a copy of *Buckingham Nicks* and played it to John and Christine to gauge their opinion. Both were impressed but didn't want to make a definite decision until they had met Lindsey and Stevie; Christine in particular was concerned about being in a band with another woman. They arranged to meet up the following evening at a Mexican restaurant in LA called El Carmen. It was a nervous encounter for all. Mick said, 'We weren't really auditioning them, they — Lindsey especially — were auditioning us.'

Thankfully, Christine's feelings about Stevie were immediately positive. She said, 'Stevie was a bright, very humorous, very direct, tough little thing. I liked her instantly, and Lindsey, too.' On New Year's Eve 1974, Mick called Lindsey and Stevie and asked them if they'd be interested in joining Fleetwood Mac.

Phew! As Mick says in his autobiography: 'I've thought about this moment many times over the years and the same feeling remains; once we sat down together at the table, I knew something was there, something was right. I knew I'd made the right choice, and because of that I could not stop smiling.'

Less than a month after Bob Welch's departure, the new Fleetwood Mac stood up and took a bow.

THEY WERE BACK IN BUSINESS.

RIGHT

Early promo shot from 1975: (L-R) John McVie, Christine McVie, Stevie Nicks, Mick Fleetwood and Lindsey Buckingham

CHAPTER 5:

RUMOURS

FLEETWOOD MAC'S PERFECT RELATIONSHIPS

Formed on New Year's Eve 1974, the new Fleetwood Mac began working almost immediately on a new album with the same eponymous title as their first LP, *Fleetwood Mac*, acknowledging, reverentially, that they had risen from the traumatic ashes which had been smouldering over the last few years.

For Lindsey and Stevie, this was a major step forward, picking up $200 a week initially — a huge pay rise at that stage in their poverty-stricken careers. Stevie even kept her job as a waitress for a few weeks because, being a thoughtful person, she didn't feel it was right to leave the restaurant in the lurch; she also wanted to be certain that the Fleetwood Mac jobs weren't just a dream and would last more than a few days. She needn't have worried; within a month their salary was increased to $800 a week; within six months she'd be rich and famous.

Rehearsals for the new line-up began in Los Angeles at the premises of their agent, International Creative Management. Right from the start, when they began to play Christine's new song, 'Say You Love Me', it was apparent that the vocal harmonies created by Lindsey, Stevie and Christine were as near to perfect as any of them could have dreamed. Although Lindsey had to adapt the way he played guitar, it was soon clear that he relished this opportunity to work with a rhythm section as good as Mick and John. The only slight issue was when Lindsey, being such a perfectionist who can play just about anything, tried to dominate the way they played their own instruments. While Mick was prepared to put up with it, John soon made his feelings clear: "I'm McVie," said John. "The band you're in is Fleetwood Mac. I'm the Mac. And I play the bass."

Lindsey never brought the issue up again. Instead, the two bands merged and became one, and the result was something very special.

Christine, Lindsey and Stevie began to write new material, but there were also several existing songs that fitted the bill perfectly. Rehearsals flowed so well that, by February '75, they were ready to go into Sound City studios and start recording with sound engineer Keith Olsen, working long hours and living on a diet of cocaine and booze. Despite such an unhealthy work environment, everything went well. The album was finished by June '75 and released the following month.

Mick was so convinced that *Fleetwood Mac* would be a great success that he paid a visit to Mo Ostin, the president of Warner Bros, and persuaded him to add another 50,000 copies to the initial manufacturing run. Ostin wasn't so sure — this band hadn't even performed live as yet — but was prepared to trust Mick's level of confidence. To prove it, Mick arranged for a short US tour with the first gig at El Paso in Texas on 15 May 1975. They tried out some old material, such as Peter Green's 'Oh Well', and various numbers from *Kiln House* to win the crowd over, and then hit them with songs from the new LP: 'Rhiannon', 'Crystal' and 'Blue Letter'; the audience loved them and every aspect of the new band — especially Stevie's voice, her clothes and stage presence. A very early concert on 5 October 1975 at the Capital Centre in Largo, Maryland is still available. The recording is not top quality and the band a little rough in places, but the raw energy on stage is remarkable.

Lindsey Buckingham's guitar playing was also inspirational. As Mick Fleetwood said in an interview with *The Irish Times*, when he first saw Lindsey perform, he identified the same level of genius he had previously seen in Peter Green. "They had the same essence but with very different forms of expression. In both I recognised that quality in artists who have mastered their instrument to such an extent that they begin to create a sound unique only to them."

RIGHT

Stevie Nicks performing at the Oakland Coliseum, California, in 1977

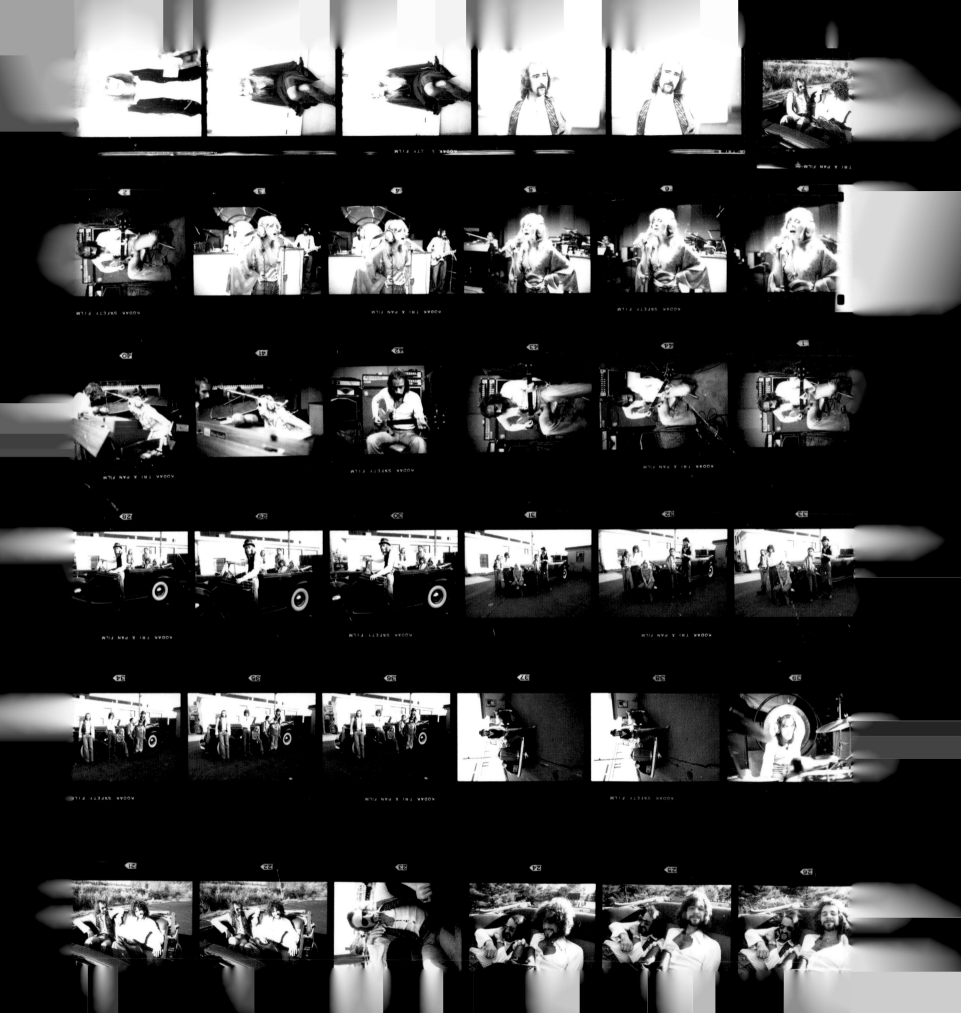

ABOVE AND LEFT

ABOVE AND RIGHT

One of Mick's great loves, vintage cars, with the band outside
Sound City studios

As usual, American FM radio stations selected tracks from *Fleetwood Mac* and played them to death over several months. But, unlike Fleetwood Mac's previous albums, which would normally then tail off, this one didn't. It was a slow burner and kept on selling steadily; by September 1976, after 56 weeks in the US charts, it reached No. 1. It even made it to No. 23 in the UK — their first British chart success since *Kiln House* in 1970. Eventually the LP sold over 5million copies, plus three singles from it ('Over My Head', 'Rhiannon' and 'Say You Love Me') all making it to the US Top 20.

But success doesn't always bring happiness. Once the album was completed, the band set off on two more American tours — the first through to the end of '75, and then, in 1976, as *Fleetwood Mac* continued to creep towards No. 1, a much bigger tour supporting the Eagles. During that same period, in February 1976, they also went into the Plant Studios in Sausalito, near San Francisco, to begin work on a new album. After a period of more than a year being either on tour or working on their first album together, the band's personal relationships were all teetering on the brink of disaster. As Mick Fleetwood put it:

"By the time we got to Sausalito to start *Rumours*, the rollercoaster was in motion. Two challenges: one was a musical challenge — another FM album — and another was knowing what was going on personally — everyone was splitting up; Lindsey and Stevie were like a married couple, and John and Christine were married. Kaboom!"

Mick had now assumed the role as Fleetwood Mac's manager and was more focused on band business than he was on his family. They had moved to a new house in the Topanga suburb of Los Angeles in the Santa Monica Mountains, about one hour's drive from the city. It was a nice location but, with Mick rarely there and Jenny increasingly being left on her own with their two children, she was soon lonelier, and unhappier, than ever.

John and Christine's marriage had been rocky for some time and his drinking had worsened to such an extent that she couldn't cope with it anymore. She could barely tolerate being in the same room as him — something of a problem, given that Mick had booked the small recording rooms at Plant Studios, and its

attached accommodation facilities, for nine weeks. As Stevie Nicks said: "I thought we would never get through *Rumours*. In that small room there were five people breaking up."

It had also become apparent to everyone, somewhat surprisingly, that Stevie and Lindsey were also having issues, caused largely by the negative effect success can impose on a relationship. Before joining Fleetwood Mac, Lindsey had very much been the dominant force within their personal and working relationship. Following the band's rapid success and the audience recognition of Stevie's unique centre stage performances, her confidence and independence blossomed. Lindsey's control over Stevie had diminished and he found that difficult to come to terms with.

One helpful solution, at Sausalito at least, was for Stevie and Christine to rent apartments at the nearby marina, while the male band members plus sound engineers Richard Dashut and Ken Caillat made use of the studio's attached accommodation. Oh how those nine weeks must have flown by… It proved to be nine weeks of turmoil; work would not start properly until the early hours of the morning, by which time they were all so high on drugs and drink that there was little point carrying on. "The sessions were like a cocktail party every night," said Christine. For the sound engineers it was terribly frustrating — all they could do was to record the snatches of decent material whenever possible and use them to put together the backing tracks.

After nine weeks, Mick recognised that there was little point in carrying on at Sausalito so took the band out on a short tour to get their breath back; Mick was very much the man in the middle and was being viewed as some sort of Fleetwood Mac marriage counselor, despite the fact that he was divorcing Jenny. On top of all their other problems, Mick found out that she had been having an affair with one of his best friends, Andy Silvester — the bass player from Chicken Shack. He and Jenny divorced in 1976 but would remarry four months later.

Mick described being in Fleetwood Mac as "more like being in group therapy!" Christine McVie had been having an affair with Fleetwood Mac's lighting director Curry Grant, who was

RIGHT

Perfect relationship: Stevie Nicks and Christine McVie cosy up in Sound City studios

John McVie, Stevie Nicks perform onstage, 1977, in Oakland,
California. It was John who came up with the title, *Rumours*

ABOVE AND RIGHT

Fleetwood Mac, 1976

then sacked at John's insistence. John was involved with Peter Green's old girlfriend, Sandra Elsdon. A month after finishing with Lindsey Buckingham, Stevie Nicks started seeing the drummer from the Eagles, Don Henley, who they'd toured with that year. And Lindsey, now footloose and fancy free, was playing the field. But somehow, these disastrous relationships combined to produce creative perfection.

As Christine McVie said: "We were all writing songs about each other, although we were unaware of this at the time. All the songs were about our own private and troubled relationships… The only thing that kept us together was the music… We were looking for a good name for the album that would encompass all that, and the feeling that the band had given up (the most active rumour flying about). And I believe it was John, one day, who said we should call it *Rumours*."

After the short tour the band headed back to the studio — not to the Plant Studios in Sausalito but to the Record Plant in Los Angeles, where it was up to the technical skills of Richard Dashut and Ken Caillat to rescue what Richard described as "a true aural collage" of "the best pieces assembled". From that point on it was rare for all five members of the band to be in the studio at the same time. Instead another three months were spent laying down individual overdubs before they began mixing and editing each track for another five months. It was painstaking, hard work. Some of the Sausalito tapes were actually damaged by the amount of times they had been used for recording. A specialist engineer from ABC/Dunhill Records had to be brought in to rescue them.

Understandably Warner Bros were concerned about the amount of money being spent and why the new album was taking so long; it was already way past its scheduled release date of September '76. Once again it was down to Mick to reassure them that everything was going to plan and the album would be worth waiting for. It was also good news for everyone that the slow burning *Fleetwood Mac* was still selling well. If they'd released *Rumours* on time, sales of the previous LP would have been badly affected.

To appease Warner Bros, Lindsey and Mick paid them a visit and convinced them that they should release an early single from *Rumours* as a teaser, to reassure the public that this delayed

album was something special. Mo Ostin wasn't convinced, fearful it could damage potential sales, but once he heard 'Go Your Own Way', he changed his mind immediately. Released in December 1976, the single made it to No. 10 in the USA, No. 38 in the UK and was a Top 20 hit across most of Europe. The teaser single proved to be the perfect trailer for *Rumours*, which was finally released on 4 February 1977.

In *Melody Maker*, Mick Fleetwood said, "This album reflects every trip and breakup. It isn't a concept thing, but when we sat down listening to what we had, we realised every track was written about someone in the band. Introspective and interesting, kind of like a soap opera. The album will show sides of people in this group that were never exposed before."

This had become a *worldwide* soap opera. *Rumours* achieved the highest pre-orders for an LP ever — 800,000 copies. Within a year of its launch date, the album had sold over 10million copies, achieving No. 1 in the USA, UK, Canada, Australia, New Zealand, South Africa and the Netherlands. Of its 11 tracks, seven were released as A- and B-sides on singles, all making it to the Top 10 in the USA. In the UK the album remained in the charts for over nine years. Based on the official sales figures of over 28million copies, it was the most successful LP of all time until *Thriller* by Michael Jackson was released in 1982. *Rumours* won a bucketful of awards and an even bigger bucketful of cash. Shopping trips for big houses, big cars and big boats took up most of whatever free time they had.

"Money is great, but it's not important," said Mick Fleetwood in *New Musical Express* in April '77. "It's not what really matters. If it had been, we would have given up long ago. It is important to maintain the right kind of motivation — and the more successful you become, the more difficult it gets.

"It may be difficult for someone outside of the group to understand what I'm saying, but we're a bunch of people before we're a bunch of musicians. What happened was that all five of us were going through exactly the same problem at the very same time. Only in Fleetwood Mac could that ever happen.

"So there we all were, trying to put down the basic backing tracks and all feeling so desperately unhappy with life. But somehow we created a mutual bond. We could all relate to each other's desperation."

Desperation has produced some of the world's greatest art. Christine McVie studied sculpture at art college and will almost certainly know the quote from the famous US sculptor, Louise Nevelson: "Most artists create out of despair. The very nature of creation is not a performing glory on the outside, it's a painful, difficult search within."

Rumours had certainly proved very painful and difficult, but few would disagree that it's up there with the greatest rock albums of all time.

FOLLOW THAT.

LEFT

Mick Fleetwood onstage playing a talking drum, reflecting his love of African music

CHAPTER 6:

FROM TUSK TO TANGO

FLEETWOOD MAC'S CHANGES IN DIRECTION

In the spring of 1976, following the debacle with Clifford Davis and the fake Fleetwood Mac, Mick Fleetwood and John McVie formed their own management company called, no doubt as a way of reflecting their opinion of previous issues, Seedy Management. One aspect of the new company was Penguin Promotions, which would handle all future Fleetwood Mac tours.

At the end of February 1977, once *Rumours* was launched, Penguin Promotions kickstarted the biggest world tour Fleetwood Mac had ever undertaken. It began with a month in the USA followed by a month in the UK and Europe and then five more months across America before heading into the southern hemisphere for a month across New Zealand and Australia and up to Japan for one week before returning home via Hawaii. Eight months on tour. After a few weeks off and some time working on new material for the next album, the band then headed off for another two months, called the 'Penguin Country Summer Safari', performing across the USA yet again. Stress levels were extreme, especially for Lindsey whose performances had reached a level more akin to personal exorcism; in July 1978 he collapsed in the shower in his hotel room in Philadelphia and was discovered unconscious by his current girlfriend, Carol Ann Harris, and rushed to hospital. He was later diagnosed as having a mild form of epilepsy and has been taking medication to control it ever since.

Mick and Jenny had been divorced in the autumn of 1976 but, four months later, remarried. It was the first (seemingly) positive event in any of the band's personal lives for years. A few months later, in November 1977, just before setting off to New

Zealand towards the end of their mammoth world tour, Mick ignited the spark of a dormant affair with Stevie Nicks that had apparently been bubbling away beneath the surface for quite some time — despite the fact that he was married to Jenny for the second time, and Stevie was still in a relationship with Don Henley. The pain and despair that had helped to create *Rumours* resurfaced and erupted. Within a year Mick and Jenny would be divorced for the second time, Christine would end her relationship with Curry Grant and begin a new one with the Beach Boys' drummer, Dennis Wilson, John would marry his secretary Julie Reubens, and Mick would have an affair with Stevie's best friend, Sara Recor; the new season in the world's biggest ever rock soap opera had begun.

While the band had been recording *Rumours* and then touring the world, the music scene across the USA and UK also changed dramatically as a result of the ideas of 1970s' youth. Punk. Sick of world politics and racial conflict and even sicker of predictable pop culture full of rock dinosaurs and prog rock pomposity, the punk anti-establishment mentality wanted to rebel against just about everything (*"whaddaya got?"* as Marlon Brando said in the 1953 classic movie, *The Wild One*).

Once again the music industry needed a kick-start. Punk, just like skiffle, stripped down to the basics, resulted in some of the most exciting music and performers for a long time. The Sex Pistols, the Clash, the Ramones, XTC, Talking Heads, the Stooges, Elvis Costello, the New York Dolls, the Jam, Patti Smith… great stuff that blew rock wide open once again and inspired many established musicians who recognised the excitement and closer links to the blues than '70s soft rock.

RIGHT

Band portrait 1976, John's appearance reflecting his love of cute penguins, among other things…

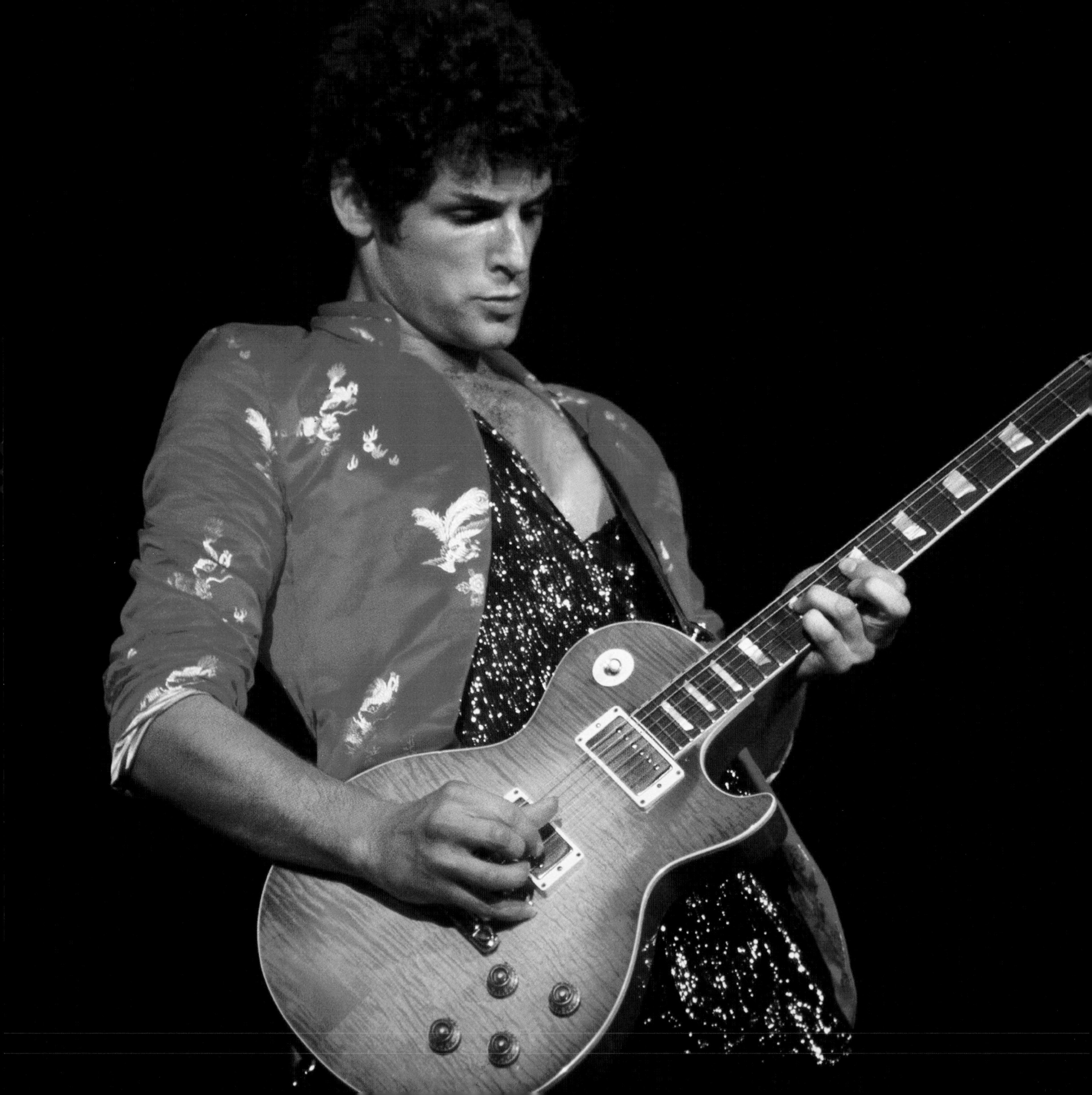

They loved it, and Lindsey Buckingham was one of them.

How to follow *Rumours*? For *Tusk*, Fleetwood Mac's answer was … punk … plus a 112-strong University of Southern California Trojan Marching Band recorded live at the LA Dodgers baseball stadium, just to maintain a little bit of rock pomposity alongside it.

Lindsey's main influence in his younger days had been the Kingston Trio, an energetic folk group from his hometown of San Francisco, so it was a surprise when fans heard he'd been watching various new wave bands perform in London. In an interview with Patrick Berkery in *Magnet* magazine in 2008, he admitted he couldn't really remember who: "I can't say I do, but man, I sure wish I'd seen the Clash back then. Bands like that played a role in the motivation behind *Tusk*. There was the reaction to avoid making *Rumours* II. But there was the fact that there was a ton of new stuff coming out that felt closer to my heart. It was ballsier, it was chancier. It felt more in the spirit of what rock'n' roll began as. That helped to inspire the confidence to do *Tusk*. It was the beginning of everything for me."

Work on *Tusk* got underway in May 1978 and Mick Fleetwood had already decided it would be a double album with so many possible tracks from their three songwriters all fighting for inclusion. Realising a double album would cost a fortune to record, Mick even suggested to Warner Bros that they build their own studio, but the idea was turned down. Instead, with the financial support of Jordy Hormel, who owned the building housing the Village Recorder studios in LA, they renovated Studio D in keeping with a design specified by Mick, Lindsey and engineers Richard Dashut and Ken Calliat.

Ironically, after all the work on Studio D, Lindsey wanted to stick to his new wave muse and record a lot of material at home by himself, then bring it in to Studio D for overdubs. The others weren't too keen, especially John McVie who laid down his bass lines early in the proceedings and then disappeared for several weeks to sail his boat to Tahiti. In effect, *Tusk* became largely a Lindsey Buckingham solo album, writing nine of the 20 songs and spending many long hours working as the main producer.

Lindsey had said he wanted to "shake people's preconceptions about pop". He certainly did. By the time *Tusk* was released in October 1979, it had cost no less than $1.4million, making it the most expensive album ever recorded at that time.

So was it, is it, any good? Warner Bros executives certainly weren't too impressed, especially when it only sold 4million copies. It made it to No. 1 in the UK, where its new wave approach was perhaps better understood, but only No. 4 in the USA. Critically the reviews were very mixed and the other band members weren't too keen either at the time, but seem to have warmed to it over the last 30 years. Mick Fleetwood, for example, says it was "way ahead of its time" and easily his second favourite Fleetwood Mac LP after *Then Play On*.

Unlike the last two LPs, however, it did start to tail off after eight months and only two of the four singles released from it sold very well. For those who didn't like it at all, of which there were many, the blame was placed squarely on Lindsey's shoulders. Although, in response, he's admitted that he might have been a little bit selfish in his approach to *Tusk*, he has always valiantly defended its artistic qualities. In *Rolling Stone* magazine as recently as 2013 he said: "It was a stand for art and for spontaneity and for the left side of the palette. I would have liked to have been a fly on the wall when Warner Bros put that on in their boardroom and listened to it for the first time. Over time it has been vindicated as a piece of work. It has become a darling for the indie bands, or at least the mentality of what that represents."

The *Tusk* tour got underway in October 1979 and was even bigger than the previous one for *Rumours*, taking up the best part of a year with the addition of more musicians, a bigger crew, a private jet, their own caterers, medical staff, security and lots and lots of cocaine. They needed it — the shows were massive and described as the nearest thing to Beatlemania the USA had seen for almost 20 years, performing to an average audience of around 15,000 fans each night.

Many of the concerts were recorded, something the band had being doing on and off since 1975 and which resulted in the release, in December 1980, of another double album,

Fleetwood Mac Live. A decent representation of the staggering amount of live shows they'd performed across the world over the last five years, the highlight, for many, was the inclusion of Peter Green's 'Oh Well', with a great trio performance from Lindsey, John and Mick. The live album made it to No. 14 in the USA and No. 31 in the UK.

To perform with such vigour after so many years on the road was incredible, so it was no surprise that, when the *Tusk* tour was completed in September 1980, they were exhausted and needed time to recover. As Mick said in *Play On*, "The end of the *Tusk* tour was the end of an era. We needed a rest and some of us — Stevie and Lindsey mostly — needed a hiatus from the band in every way. Each of them had plans for solo projects..."

Lindsey and Stevie were also distancing themselves from Fleetwood Mac in other ways. Both were now represented by outside organisations — not Mick and John's Seedy Management — and there were questions being raised as to where all the money from the *Tusk* tour had gone. Mick blamed it on tour expenses and, in his defense, argued that he and tour manager, John Courage, had tried to cut corners but no one else would accept it. They wouldn't accept that excuse either and Mick was relieved of his position as the band's manager, while John Courage was released as tour manager. It was also decided that there'd be a nine-month Fleetwood Mac sabbatical to allow everyone to take a step back and pursue other interests.

Ironically it was Mick who was the first to bring out a solo LP, *The Visitor*, recorded in Ghana in 1981 and released by RCA in June that year. A reflection of his love of Africa, Mick persuaded RCA to finance the project using mainly local musicians combined with help from George Harrison and Peter Green. It's a surprisingly good album that merits comparison with Paul Simon's *Graceland* five years later but which, unsurprisingly, sold very few copies.

Stevie Nick's first solo LP, *Bella Donna*, was released a month later and, equally unsurprisingly, went straight to No. 1 in the US and No. 11 in the UK. She had been working on solo material

LEFT

John McVie reaches out to the crouching Stevie Nicks. Lindsey Buckingham looks on from across the stage

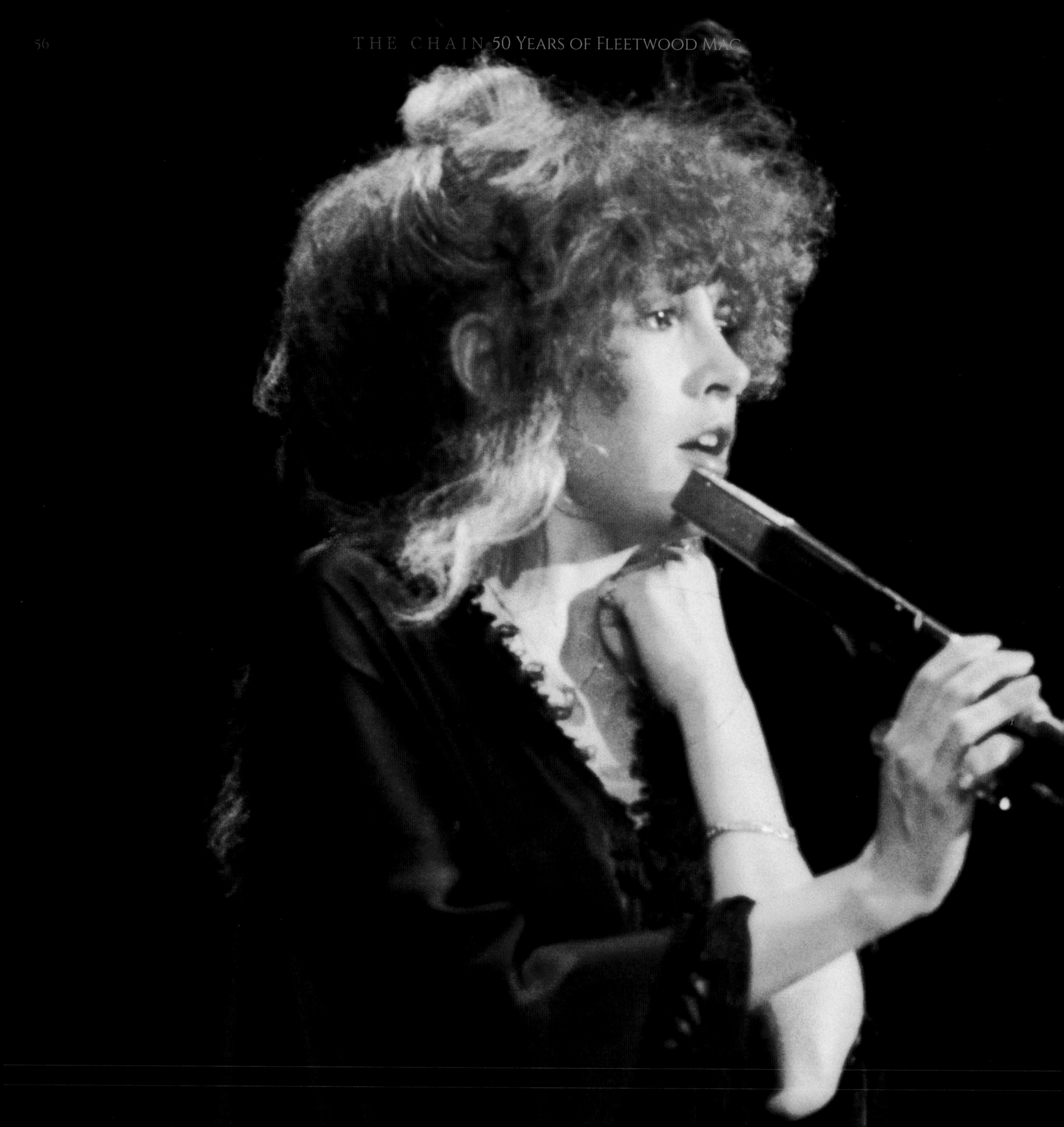

for the last couple of years and had formed her own record company, Modern Records, as early as 1976. By 1980 she had plenty of songs to choose from. Produced and recorded with Jimmy Iovine and Tom Petty and the Heartbreakers, plus Don Henley on drums and vocals, backing vocalists Lori Perry and Sharon Celani, and a number of top session musicians, Stevie proved (as if she needed to) that she was capable of functioning very well with or without Fleetwood Mac.

Three months later, Lindsey Buckingham's *Law and Order* was released with Lindsey playing most of the instruments himself, with backing from Mick Fleetwood, Christine McVie and Carol Ann Harris, his girlfriend for the last three years. With the same stripped down, home studio approach as Lindsey's production on *Tusk*, the album has its moments and made it to No. 32 in the US but is not generally regarded as his finest work.

Following the sabbatical, Fleetwood Mac were back in the studio in May 1981 but, for the first time since 1973, outside the USA, at Le Chateau d'Herouville near Paris — the studio where Elton John recorded his album *Honky Chateau*. There must have been some sighs of relief when Stevie turned up, given the huge success of *Bella Donna*, but the few months break had clearly been reinvigorating for all of them. The financial concerns at the end of the *Tusk* tour, and the switch to new management, meant there was less time or money to waste. They knuckled down and got on with the job and the basic

tracks were all laid down within a couple of months.

Lindsey had clearly also been ordered not to even think about heading down the *Tusk* new wave route (which had moved on by 1981 anyway), so the next album, *Mirage*, saw the band all working together in the studio and all getting on well. Once the basic tracks were in the bag, the band headed back to Larrabee Sound and the Record Plant studios in LA to take care of the overdubs and mixing, with Richard Dashut and Ken Caillat in charge.

Released in June 1982, *Mirage* was generally well-received, reaching No. 1 in the US and No. 5 in the UK, but there was also a general feeling that the new LP was a little lacklustre and disappointing. "We should have progressed, but instead we just reacted against *Tusk*," said Lindsey Buckingham. "It was pleasant but much too safe." In a newspaper interview, Christine agreed, "We had decided we'd go in and do something that was expected from us, and it failed. From our points of view, I think I can say that we were all disappointed. It reeks of insincerity to me." She added, in an attempt to explain what had gone wrong: "*Rumours* had been born out of strife and tensions. During the recording of *Mirage* the band members were boringly friendly again. We were no longer the musical soap opera we used to be!"

A short tour to promote *Mirage* followed and everything seemed to be just so … nice and cosy. But, however happy everyone appeared to be, it would be five more years until it was time to...

... TANGO IN THE NIGHT.

Stevie Nicks performing her first solo LP, *Bella Donna*, 1981

CHAPTER 7:

FROM TANGO TO TIME

FLEETWOOD MAC'S WILDERNESS YEARS, PART 2

There was plenty of time to make use of over the next five years until *Tango in the Night* would finally arrive. After a very short tour (by their standards) to promote *Mirage*, both Lindsey and Stevie made it clear that they didn't want to tour anymore, but stay at home and work on new songs … but not for Fleetwood Mac. Both had another solo album in the pipeline. But what had seemed an open book that would allow all of them to devote more time to their own lives and projects was immediately impacted by personal problems and tragic events.

Stevie Nicks had been struggling with drink and drug problems for some time but, in 1981, her best friend since school days, Robin Snyder, was diagnosed with leukemia. Robin lived in LA and worked for Stevie's Modern Records, where she met and started dating one of Warner Bros' promotions staff, Kim Anderson. After being diagnosed, Robin and Kim got married and, in October 1982, she gave birth to a baby boy, Matthew. Tragically, Robin died just two days later. Grieving deeply and doing what they felt was best for baby Matthew, Stevie and Kim were married in January 1983. It was a brave step but not the wisest. Amid an atmosphere of shocked reaction from many friends and relatives, Stevie and Kim realised they had made a mistake and were divorced within three months. Stevie has remained close to both Kim and Matthew.

The other band members also had to deal with various personal issues. John McVie was used to being the quiet one in the background or sailing his yacht these days, but in 1981 had hit the headlines when his house in Hawaii was raided by the police. A sniffer dog had detected cocaine in a parcel to their home, where the police also found several illegal handguns and rifles. John claimed he knew nothing about the cocaine and passed a lie-detector test to support his statement. The police also charged his wife, Julie, with hindering the prosecution by trying to destroy some of the evidence. They faced the possibility of being deported, but in the end John was fined $1,000 and Julie given a warning.

Lindsey Buckingham had split with his girlfriend Carol Ann Harris after more than six years together, while Mick Fleetwood was now in a relationship with Sara Recor, but was having to deal with severe financial problems. He had spent a fortune on drugs and even more on property investments that all seemed to have collapsed and turned to dust. Twice, in 1981 and 1984, he had no choice but to walk away and face bankruptcy.

These had not been easy times for any of them during this second period of wilderness years, but it did see the creation of five more solo albums that, as before, achieved mixed levels of success.

Mick once again was the first to stick his toe into the solo pool with *I'm Not Me*, produced in Malibu and LA by Richard Dashut and performed by what had become his own band, Mick Fleetwood's Zoo, featuring Billy Burnette on guitar/vocals, Steve Ross on guitar/vocals and George Hawkins on bass/vocals. Lindsey Buckingham and Christine McVie also contributed. Released in May 1983, it's typical '80s middle of the road rock but sold very few copies.

RIGHT

Mick Fleetwood performs in Ghana, Africa, 1980

The next month saw the release of Stevie Nick's second solo LP, *The Wild Heart*, again featuring Tom Petty and the Heartbreakers plus Mick Fleetwood and a few dozen other musicians including Prince (uncredited) and backing vocalists Lori Perry and Sharon Celani, who have been with Stevie ever since. Lori married Stevie's brother, Christopher, and is known as Lori Nicks, although they are now divorced. Released in June '83, *The Wild Heart* was very well-received, as expected, and made it to No. 5 in the US charts. It was the nearest to a Fleetwood Mac LP fans would see for another four years.

Christine's second solo LP, simply called *Christine McVie* in keeping with 1970's *Christine Perfect*, arrived in January 1984. Recorded in Switzerland and England, Christine had sufficient pulling power to bring in Eric Clapton, Steve Winwood, percussionist Ray Cooper and the Average White Band's drummer, Steve Ferrone, plus Mick and some of his Zoo crew. The album reached No. 26 in the US and No. 58 in the UK and was liked by many, but reviewers sensed it lacked variety and the spark of Fleetwood Mac.

Lindsey Buckingham's second solo effort, *Go Insane*, was put together while he was dealing with the end of his six-year relationship with Carol Ann Harris. Flicking through Harris's kiss-and-tell book, *Storms: My Life with Lindsey Buckingham and Fleetwood Mac*, gives you an idea of where she's coming from. He did, however, dedicate the LP to her. Once again Lindsey played the majority of the instruments himself, recorded at Cherokee Studios in LA and his home studio. The LP did reasonably well, reaching No. 49 in the US.

Stevie's third solo LP, *Rock A Little* finally arrived in November '85, about a year later than planned. She'd been unhappy with the early mixes from Jimmy Iovine who had produced *The Wild Heart* and her first solo LP, *Bella Donna*, during which time a relationship blossomed. Having worked with the likes of John Lennon, Bruce Springsteen, Tom Petty, Patti Smith and Meat Loaf, Iovine was regarded as one of the best producers in the country, but his relationship with Stevie had come to an end after *Bella Donna*.

The project was scrapped and reinitiated with Keith Olsen —

the man who had produced the LPs *Buckingham Nicks* and *Fleetwood Mac* at Sound City in LA and as a result gone on to produce the Grateful Dead, Emerson, Lake and Palmer, Jefferson Starship, Santana, Foreigner, Whitesnake… At one time he had employed Stevie at Sound City as a cleaner. How their lives had changed in the last 10 years. *Rock A Little* reached No. 12 in the US charts but overall was something of a disappointment. Very '80s with big drums, big synthesizers and big hair.

Many of Stevie's problems at that time were the result of her increasing addictions to alcohol and cocaine, with the result that as soon as she'd finished a six-month tour in '86 to promote *Rock A Little*, she checked into the Betty Ford Center in California. She said: "I've always been anti-drugs, but I thought drink was harmless, just a relaxation. I can't tell you how wrong I was. I have to tell you that the Betty Ford people were marvelous."

Now describing herself as "strictly an orange juice girl", Stevie blames most of her problems on her unhealthy devotion to the band: "I guess I got paranoid about the way Fleetwood Mac simply died. I couldn't understand it. We'd been one of the hottest properties for years, but suddenly it all fell apart when the others wanted to start doing their own thing. I recorded a couple of solo albums, but I was always aching to get working with the Mac again."

An interesting view, given that it was Stevie who'd recorded three solo records, spent months on tour and was the most difficult one to entice back into the Fleetwood Mac fold to record *Tango in the Night*. It was actually Christine who brought them back together when she recorded a song for the soundtrack of the film, *A Fine Mess*. The song she was asked to cover was 'Can't Help Falling in Love', originally recorded by Elvis Presley. She knew Lindsey and sound engineer Richard Dashut were both big Elvis fans and asked them to produce it, so it seemed sensible to invite Mick and John to be the rhythm section.

Stevie was in the middle of her *Rock A Little* tour at that stage and so did not arrive at the *Tango in the Night* studio sessions until January 1987, but contributed three tracks to add to Christine and Lindsey's nine songs. Two of those were co-written by Christine and her new husband, Eddy Quintela,

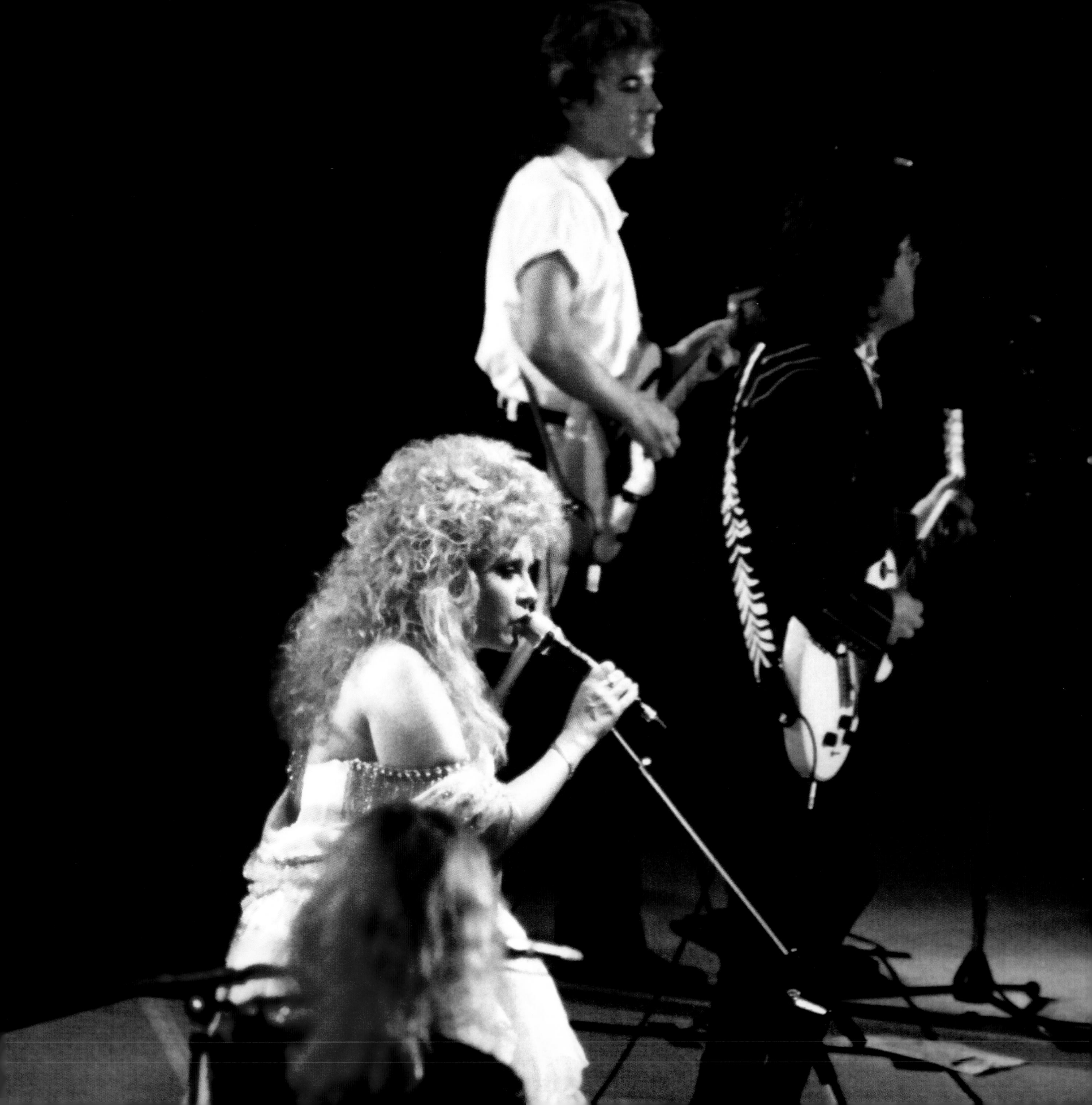

a keyboard player who'd she'd met in Switzerland when he performed on her *Christine McVie* solo album. They tied the knot in October 1986.

As always, recording the new LP proved far from easy; "like pulling teeth" was how Mick described it. Produced by Lindsey and Richard Dashut at Rumbo Recorders in LA and at Lindsey's home studio (now extended and given the title 'the Slope') most of the problems were caused by the fact they had barely played together for four years, had no real management in place and were finding it increasingly hard to get Stevie into the studio at all, let alone perform.

It was a slow, painful process, taking more than 18 months to record. By then, five years since *Mirage* had been released, there were concerns people might have lost interest in Fleetwood Mac. As Christine put it, "Five years in this business is almost the kiss of death."

She needn't have worried. Once again, desperation was the key to creativity. Just about everyone loved it. Released in April 1987, *Tango in the Night* leapt up the charts to No. 1 in the UK and No. 7 in the US. Of the four singles lifted from it, three in the UK and two in the US were Top 10 hits. The album has sold over 7million copies and is regarded by many as their second best LP after *Rumours*.

To celebrate and promote such success, of course, Fleetwood Mac would normally set off on another mammoth world tour, but Lindsey Buckingham made it clear he didn't want to. In *Magnet*

magazine, he said, "The time right after *Mirage* and through *Tango In The Night* was just the craziest time as far as the band goes. The lack of discipline, the personal habits, the alienation, everything. Making *Tango*, which was largely done in my garage, was almost impossible. Out of a year of working, we probably saw Stevie for maybe three weeks. It was smoke and mirrors. At the end of that album, I just couldn't contemplate going out on the road with that. That was the beginning of me trying to pull back and regain some of my sense of self and sanity."

The other band members tried to persuade him to change his mind and, for a short period of time, he agreed to tour for 10 weeks, but then changed his mind again. Tour dates and rehearsals had already been set up; the band were livid and demanded he come to a meeting at Christine's house to explain himself. In such a tinderbox of emotion it was no surprise the meeting turned into a full-blown argument, which became physical between Lindsey and Stevie. It's reported that he slapped and pushed her and had to be restrained by Stevie's manager. Lindsey soon issued a press statement announcing he had left Fleetwood Mac.

Yet again, the band needed a replacement guitarist. In fact, it was decided that no one on their own could match Lindsey's level of intensity in a live performance, so they went on the search for two. Billy Burnette, who had played on Mick's solo LP, *I'm Not Me*, was the first to spring to mind. Not only was he thrilled to be asked, he also had a good friend called Rick Vito who'd played with performers such as Bob Seeger, Dolly Parton, Bonnie Rait, Jackson Browne, Delaney & Bonnie, and even with John McVie

L-R Stevie Nicks, Rick Vito and Billy Burnette performing at Wembley Arena, London, June 1988

back in the '70s when they had both got together with John Mayall for a short time. He was the perfect choice for the role as second guitar and, with musicians of such high calibre, it didn't take them long to get up to speed. The new line-up set off on Fleetwood Mac's 'Shake the Cage' tour in September 1987.

Through to the end of '87 and into early '88 the tour went incredibly well — no one seemed to even miss Lindsey. The only negative aspect of the whole tour was that by March Stevie was suffering with a poor throat, which meant the Australian leg of the tour had to be cancelled and the European dates reduced and rescheduled. Apart from that disappointment, the tour continued through to the end of June '88 and was a huge success.

The band's second *Greatest Hits* LP, covering only the hits from the Buckingham-Nicks period plus two new songs, came out in November '88 and went to No. 3 in the UK and No. 14 in the US. It had been a particularly good year for Mick, as well, when he married his long-term girlfriend, Sara Recor, on 24 April. The 200-plus superstar guest list included all of Fleetwood Mac (with John as best man), plus Bob Dylan, George Harrison, Jeff Lynne and many more. Best of all was that Lindsey Buckingham turned up unannounced and some of the emotional scars were able to heal. John McVie also enjoyed a special year in 1989 when he became a father for the first time at the age of 43. Julie gave birth to Molly Elizabeth at Cedars-Sinai Hospital in LA on 28 February. He had given up drinking in 1987 when he suffered an alcohol-induced seizure. He hasn't drunk alcohol ever since.

They then began working on new material for their next LP, *Behind the Mask*, with recording getting underway at the Complex in LA in 1989. Everyone was getting on really well, especially Stevie with Rick Vito and Billy Burnette, who had started to write together. Said Stevie: "I love nothing more than when Billy and Ricky show up at my house with a guitar. A lot of that goes on now, and it hasn't gone on for 12 years since Lindsey and I split up. We actually sit around and play music. I love that."

Behind the Mask was released in April 1990 and made it to No. 18 in the US but straight to No. 1 in the UK, where their popularity seemed to be growing every day. New members Burnette and Vito had credits on no less than eight of the album's 13 tracks, having written with Stevie, Christine and various other outside composers. Christine had also co-written two songs with husband Eddy Quintela. With six band members and four songwriters, this was the most varied and collaborative album of the later Fleetwood Mac's 15 years together and, although not everyone rated it very highly, others loved it. *Rolling Stone* magazine referred to the two new band members as "the best thing to ever happen to Fleetwood Mac". The band toured from May through to December 1990 and even Lindsey Buckingham got up and played with them at the last show in LA.

Once again, everything seemed so warm and cosy but, as usual, it wasn't. Not long after the tour finished, first Christine, then Stevie, then Rick Vito, then Billy Burnette...

... ALL DECIDED THEY'D HAD ENOUGH OF FLEETWOOD MAC.

RIGHT

Mick Fleetwood , 1990

CHAPTER 8:

SAY YOU WILL

FLEETWOOD MAC BORN AGAIN

Before being born again, Fleetwood Mac had to die. And die they did, soon after the *Behind the Mask* tour came to an end in December 1990. Almost immediately, three members of the band announced they would no longer be touring with Fleetwood Mac, although initially Stevie Nicks and Christine McVie said they would continue to record with the band if a new album was planned.

Of the three, Christine had the most understandable reason for calling it a day. Her father, Cyril, had died while she was on tour in the USA. On top of her grieving, she was also physically and mentally exhausted and decided there were more important things in life to worry about. Rick Vito had reached a similar conclusion and left the band for "personal reasons" and to concentrate on his first solo LP, *King of Hearts*, which was released on Stevie Nicks's own label, Modern Records, in 1992.

Stevie had continued to work on her fourth solo LP, *The Other Side of the Mirror*, which was released in May 1989 and achieved reasonable success, making it to No. 3 in the UK and No. 10 in the US. Her producer, the British musician Rupert Hine, also became her partner for a short time and Stevie took the new LP on tour not just across America but also to Europe for the first time as a solo artist.

Her memories of those times, however, are extremely vague due to her use of Klonopin, a drug for the treatment of epileptic seizures and panic attacks, which she had been prescribed by a psychiatrist. After leaving the Betty Ford Center where she'd been treated for her addiction to cocaine, friends were increasingly concerned she'd start taking it again, but their well-meant concerns had led to Stevie becoming equally anxious and stressed. Her psychiatrist prescribed Klonopin for that reason, but for Stevie it proved a disaster. Although it calmed her concerns, it also affected her personality and she was left drowsy and lacking in energy. "I just stopped doing everything. I just wasn't good for anyone," said Stevie in *Mojo* magazine. "I just stayed home." Eventually she was hospitalised for more than six weeks. "I didn't leave Fleetwood Mac," she said. "My brain left me."

On top of those health issues, Stevie was also angry with Mick Fleetwood because he had signed away the rights to her song, 'Silver Springs' (a track that had not made it onto *Rumours*) for use on a new Fleetwood Mac boxset, *25 Years — The Chain*, covering the band's output from the late '60s right through to four brand new songs. Understandably, Stevie felt she should have the right to use her song on her own compilation LP, *Timespace: The Best of Stevie Nicks*, but Warner Bros refused. Furious, and in a fit of pique, Stevie said she wanted nothing more to do with Fleetwood Mac. Almost quite fittingly, it seemed that *25 Years — The Chain* had broken, and might signal the end of Fleetwood Mac.

What prevented such a sad demise, however, was a call, or possibly a demand, from on high — none other than President Clinton — for the classic line-up (Fleetwood, McVie, McVie, Buckingham, Nicks) to take to the stage and perform his favourite song, 'Don't Stop', at his Presidential Inaugural Gala Ball in January 1993. The song had been the Democrats' theme tune throughout Bill Clinton's election campaign. All were happy to oblige but their temporary reunion did not, as many had hoped, persuade them to get back together on a more permanent basis.

It did, however, encourage Mick Fleetwood to record some more Fleetwood Mac music with yet another new line-up; urgently needed were a new guitarist and a new female singer. As usual, Mick didn't find it too difficult to recruit new band members.

RIGHT

Bekka Bramlett performing with Fleetwood Mac at the Universal Ampitheatre, Los Angeles

First to take a step forward was Bekka Bramlett, the daughter of the superb country rock and soul duo, Delaney & Bonnie. All three members of the family had contributed to Mick's third solo album, *Shakin' the Cage*, released in June 1992. Credited to the Zoo, the album featured Bekka on lead vocals and Billy Burnette on guitar. At around the same time, Billy also worked on John McVie's only solo album, *John McVie's 'Gotta Band'* with Lola Thomas (an American jazz and blues singer), plus additional support from the former Rolling Stone, Mick Taylor.

All of the Fleetwood Mac band members were obviously in solo mode at that time; Stevie Nicks had completed her fifth solo LP, *Street Angels*, the least successful of her albums so far, making it to just No. 45 in the US and No. 16 in the UK charts, despite contributions from the likes of Bob Dylan, David Crosby and the Welsh guitarist, Andy Fairweather Low. With her various health problems it was not a good time for Stevie Nicks and it would be seven more years before another solo album would arrive.

In 1993, Billy Burnette decided, after all his contributions to the other band members' LPs, that he wanted to quit Fleetwood Mac as well, to concentrate on his ninth solo album, *Coming Home*. It was released that year but, in keeping with all of these latest Fleetwood Mac solo albums, produced very little in the way of critical acclaim and sold relatively few copies. In 1994, Billy contacted Mick to see if he could rejoin Fleetwood Mac; Mick was happy to welcome him back.

For the remaining empty guitar slot, Mick turned to the English musician Dave Mason, who had previously played with one of the UK's most influential bands, Traffic. Dave had left Traffic in 1968 to pursue a solo career and became part of Delaney & Bonnie and Friends, a variable rock ensemble that also included the likes of Eric Clapton, Duane and Gregg Allman, Leon Russell, Rita Coolidge, Graham Parsons and George Harrison. Bekka Bramlett was less than a year old when Dave Mason arrived on the scene, but the two got to know each other well as Bekka grew up as part of this rock 'n' roll royal family. It seemed the perfect mix for the new Fleetwood Mac line-up but, once again, things didn't work out according to plan.

With all of the Fleetwood Mac slots filled, work began on their 16th studio album, *Time*, released in October 1995. Stevie Nicks, obviously, had nothing to do with this album, but Christine McVie did at least fulfill her commitment to continue recording with the band, contributing five songs co-written with her husband Eddy Quintela. The rest were put together by Billy Burnette, Dave Mason, Bekka Bramlett, Mick Fleetwood and other songwriters in various combinations. Even Lindsey Buckingham turned up at some point to contribute backing vocals on one of the numbers.

With very little promotion from Warner Bros it was no great surprise the album was not well-received by the public or press, failing to make the charts at all in the USA and only reaching No. 47 in the UK. There was nothing really 'wrong' with the album, but it was not recognisable as Fleetwood Mac. When it came time to go on tour, Christine stuck to her decision not to go on the road with the band anymore. With five months supporting *Time* in 1994, followed by another five months in 1995 as part of a 'revival' package with REO Speedwagon and Pat Benatar, it was a tough period and something of a fall from grace for Fleetwood Mac. To make it even more of a revival, the band used it as an opportunity to revisit some of their '60s numbers, and even Jeremy Spencer performed with them one night in Tokyo.

To make matters worse over such a gruelling few months on the road, there were major problems between Bekka Bramlett and Dave Mason who, despite their long-term family connections, clearly didn't get on at all and found it difficult to work together. As Mick Fleetwood said in *Play On*: "There was real bad blood between them. As the tour wore on, I found myself having to play mediator for them almost every day. I'd completely misread what I thought would be a quaint and historically perfect collaboration." Mason didn't get on too well with Christine McVie, either.

Once the second tour came to an end, Mick's frustrated and disappointed response was to issue 'letters of disengagement' to the three latest recruits and make an official announcement that Fleetwood Mac had disbanded. This time, it seemed, their days really were over. Billy Burnette and Bekka Bramlett formed

a new country music duo, Bekka & Billy, and released an album of the same name in 1997 but split in '98. Dave Mason returned to his solo career, which he continues to this day.

Once again it was the band's links to solo albums that at least kept them all in touch. First Mick, then John, and then Christine were all called in to contribute to Lindsey Buckingham's next planned fourth solo release, *Gift of Screws*. Although the album didn't actually materialise until 2008 (because Warner Bros initially rejected it), it did lead to one or two other minor reconciliations that left them all in a positive frame of mind.

In 1997 they were offered the opportunity to record an MTV Unplugged Special. The classic line-up reformed in March '97 and two months later took part in a live recording on the Warner Bros soundstage in Burbank, California for a DVD and CD package called *The Dance*. Just over 20 years since *Rumours* had arrived, they were together again and performing as well as ever. Released in August 1997, it shot straight to No. 1 in the USA and No. 15 in the UK. After hitting the depths of failure just two years earlier, Fleetwood Mac were back in business once again.

Inevitably, the next step was a 44-show tour of the USA from September through to November 1997. As if in recognition of the last 20 years, music awards were being handed to the band on a regular basis. On 12 January 1998 all of the major

members of Fleetwood Mac (with the curious exception of Bob Welch) were inducted into the Rock & Roll Hall of Fame at the Waldorf Astoria Hotel in New York. Peter Green was even persuaded to get up on stage with Carlos Santana and perform 'Black Magic Woman'. In February, they were presented with an award for an Outstanding Contribution to the British Music Industry at the UK's Brit Awards in London and performed a medley of several of their big hits. Later that month they were nominated in three categories at the US Grammy Awards and performed the medley of hits once again.

It was a very good time for a band that had so nearly crumbled just two years earlier. As always, however, there was one disappointing note when Christine informed the band she had made the decision to leave Fleetwood Mac completely. She'd simply had enough of everything, on top of which she had developed a severe fear of flying. Touring, or even travelling to the USA to record, had become nigh on impossible. She wanted to withdraw from the music business altogether and spend more time at home in the Kentish countryside with her family.

In 1990 she had bought a six-bedroomed, Grade II-listed, 17th-century mansion called the Quaives in Wickhambreaux, near Canterbury, Kent. The rather ramshackle building had been completely renovated and she converted an old barn into a recording studio. For Christine, there was no longer any need to leave home. After leaving the band in 1998, she spent the next 16 years almost in hibernation, although she did produce her third solo album, *In the Meantime*, recorded in her studio in Kent with Ken Caillat and her nephew, Dan Perfect. Released in 2004, the album failed to chart in both the UK and USA. One song had been co-written with Eddy Quintela but, by then, her second marriage had also come to an end.

Mick had got married to Sara Recor in 1988 but it was a troubled relationship from the outset, largely due to both struggling with alcohol-related problems. Mick had met another woman, Lynn Frankel, in 1989 and they became involved romantically in 1990. Mick and Sara divorced in 1995 and he married Lynn that same year. Their twin daughters, Ruby and Tessa, were born in 2002.

LEFT

John McVie and Mick Fleetwood at a benefit for Willie Dixon's Blues Heaven Foundation, Hollywood, 1994

Stevie Nicks released a new compilation CD boxset, *Enchanted* in 1998. Her health was still not on top form but did improve sufficiently over the next couple of years to allow her to work on another solo album, *Trouble in Shangri La*, which was released by Reprise Records in 2001, reaching No. 5 in the USA and No. 43 in the UK.

Lindsey Buckingham had been working as a solo artist since leaving Fleetwood Mac in 1987 and released his third album, *Out of the Cradle*, in 1992. It made it to No. 51 in the UK but did not chart in the USA. He toured as a solo artist and worked on a fourth solo album, *Gift of Screws* from 1995—2001. More importantly, he and his partner, Kristen Messen, became first-time parents on 8 July 1998 when their son, Will was born. They were married in 2000 and a baby sister, Leelee, arrived the same year. A third child, Stella, was born in 2004.

Because Warner Bros rejected Lindsey's solo album, *Gift of Screws*, it was suggested he might want to make use of some of the tracks for a new Fleetwood Mac album; reluctantly Lindsey agreed. Mick and John joined him in Los Angeles and they worked on the new album through to November 2002, with Stevie joining them as often as she could. *Say You Will* was released in April 2003 and made it to the Top 10 in both the US (No. 3) and UK (No. 6) and was generally very well-received, although several reviewers made the point that this, in effect, was a new Buckingham-Nicks album. Although there were hopes that Christine might contribute a couple of songs, she didn't, but had at least played keyboards on two numbers recorded before she left the band. A 16-month tour to promote *Say You Will* set off across the USA, Europe and Australia through to September 2004.

What followed were five more wilderness years when the band rarely raised its head above the parapet. Solo albums once again became the routine, with two more from Lindsey Buckingham (*Under the Skin* in 2006 and a revised version of *Gift of Screws* finally arriving in 2008); another compilation album, *Crystal Visions… The Very Best of Stevie Nicks* was released in 2007; Christine McVie's *In the Meantime* in 2004;

LEFT

Lindsey Buckingham demonstrates his unique guitar technique, 2004

and the Mick Fleetwood Band's *Something Big* in 2004 followed by the *Mick Fleetwood Blues Band's Blues Again* in 2008.

Surprisingly, in March 2009, Fleetwood Mac set off on another world tour, despite the fact there was no new album to promote and Stevie Nicks had firmly stated she would not perform with the band again unless Christine McVie returned. But times, and promises often change. The band once again travelled across the USA, Australia, New Zealand and Europe. Christine turned up to watch them perform at Wembley Arena in London, as she had during the previous tour in 2003. On both occasions her attendance had been recognised by the audience with standing ovations.

London was one of the few places where she would happily pay them a visit, but anywhere further afield was still difficult. Her flying phobia had not diminished, so she decided to seek help. In one of her early psychiatric sessions with a therapist she was asked where she'd like to visit first. She replied she'd like to go to Maui to see Mick and John. The therapist told her to book a flight for six months' time and together they began working hard to conquer her fears.

In 2013, just before the six months were up, Mick flew to London for some press interviews and suggested Christine should fly back to Maui with him. She did, and loved it. So much so that, while staying in Hawaii, she got up on stage with Mick Fleetwood's Blues Band, featuring Rick Vito, and performed four numbers, including 'Don't Stop'. It was her first time on stage since 1998.

Regardless of her solitary but idyllic lifestyle in the lovely county of Kent, the truth was that Christine was already finding her life rather dull and boring. She had worked hard to transform her country manor into a stunning home in 19 acres of beautiful landscaped gardens, she enjoyed the company of her family, often enjoyed a few drinks in the local pub, did a lot of cooking and walked her dogs every day… but the truth was that she missed Fleetwood Mac. As she said in the *Sunday Times Magazine* in August 2013, her life had become "rather lonely — apart from my brother and sister-in-law I still don't know anyone down here".

The following month in September, at a Fleetwood Mac concert at the O2 Arena Christine joined the band on stage for the first time in 15 years to perform 'Don't Stop'. The audience response was emotional and rapturous. "It was like falling off a bike," said Christine. "I climbed back on there again and there they all were, the same old faces." Even Peter Green was in the audience that night.

Three months later in December, in an interview with the *Guardian*, she was asked if she'd ever considered rejoining the band. Her answer was: "If they were to ask me, I would probably be very delighted." The truth was, she already knew. The following month, in January 2014, it was announced that Christine McVie had rejoined Fleetwood Mac. In the *Sunday Times* she said she felt as if she had emerged from years of isolation and "mud, and grey days, where your life is dark, your heart is dark, your brain is dark".

For Mick, John, Lindsey, Stevie and Christine,

THE CHAIN, ONCE AGAIN, WAS UNBROKEN.

RIGHT

Fleetwood Mac, back together, performing on NBC's *Today Show*, October 2014, New York

EPILOGUE:
FUTURE GAMES
WHERE NOW FOR FLEETWOOD MAC?

Apart from Mick Fleetwood divorcing his wife Lynn in 2013, it had been a good year for Fleetwood Mac. They'd released their first record for 10 years with a new digital EP called *Extended Play*, which reached No. 48 in the US charts in its first week. Featuring three songs from Lindsey Buckingham and one from Stevie Nicks, it wasn't a new album but was generally well-received and, for the fans, better than nothing.

The best news for fans that year had been Christine McVie's return to the fold but then, a month after her first performance for 15 years at the O2 Arena, it was announced that her ex-husband John McVie had been diagnosed with colon cancer. All were devastated. The reunited band were forced to cancel various gigs in New Zealand and Australia while John underwent treatment. Thankfully, his prognosis was good and the treatment worked well — so well that the band were able to set off on yet another major excursion, the 'On With the Show' tour, beginning in Minneapolis on 30 September 2014 through to Auckland, New Zealand, on 22 November 2015. Remarkably, despite the fact the tour took in 120 shows across the USA, Canada, Europe (including the Isle of Wight Festival), Australia and New Zealand, John was able to join them. Even better, in 2017, he was given the all clear.

With such a successful tour under their belts, it was inevitable there'd be talk about the possibility of a new Fleetwood Mac album at some point in the future. In the *Guardian* in January 2015, Lindsey said that any new album might be Fleetwood Mac's swansong and that the band might cease to be soon afterwards. He concluded: "We're going to continue working on the new album, and the solo stuff will take a back seat for a year or two. A beautiful way to wrap up this last act."

Lindsey and Stevie had both produced solo material in 2011

— he with *Seeds We Sow* and Stevie with *In Your Dreams*, but she had also worked on another solo release in 2014 — *24 Karat Gold: Songs From the Vault*, featuring new versions of old songs from her 1969-87 period. Her solo career remains her priority and Mick Fleetwood has warned that any new Fleetwood Mac album might take a few years to complete because they are still waiting for her contributions, and she hasn't shown a great deal of interest.

In an interview with the *Sunday Times* in May 2015, in the middle of the 'On With the Show' tour, she was asked if she'd be keen to have any of her own material on a new Fleetwood Mac album. Her response was, "I don't know how I feel about that. I'm not in a good place right now to make decisions. We are on the road, and in my opinion we should not be thinking past that… This tour would never have happened if Chris hadn't come back."

In *Billboard* magazine in September 2016, Stevie said, "Is it possible that Fleetwood Mac might do another record? You know what, I never know what's going to happen. And I certainly didn't ever, after 16 years, think that Christine McVie was going to call up and say, 'How would you feel if I came back to the band?' You know, it's like, are you serious? Is this a joke?"

Her statement back in 2009 that she would not perform with the band unless Christine McVie returned seems, in some ways, to have backfired. Certainly there have been issues; in the *Sunday Times*, Christine revealed that when she had brought up the question of why it was taking so long to finish the album, Stevie's response had been: "You've just had 16 years off. Now it's my turn."

Studio sessions for a possible new Fleetwood Mac album actually got underway in 2014. *Billboard* magazine revealed

RIGHT
_____

Mick Fleetwood performs onstage during the Classic East —
Day 2, at Citi Field, July 2017, New York

that the band had already spent two months in Studio D at the Village Recorder in Los Angeles, but without Stevie Nicks. Recording was then put on hold while the band prepared for their 'On With the Show' tour.

In 2015 Stevie announced that she was ready to start working with the band in the studio, but then changed her mind and concentrated on touring her latest *24 Karat Gold* solo album. She may well have been unhappy with the fact that, when Christine McVie had rejoined the band, she had brought with her a hoard of new material. As Mick Fleetwood told *Classic Rock*: "I do know that when Christine came back, she came back with a bag full of goods. She and Lindsey could probably have a mighty strong duet album if they want."

And that, of course, is what Lindsey and Christine decided to do — to go their own way, with help from Mick Fleetwood and John McVie, and release the album as a duo, rather than wait for

Stevie Nicks to make herself available. The new album *Lindsey Buckingham/Christine McVie* arrived in June 2107 just as this book was going to print.

As Christine McVie told *Billboard* magazine in January 2017: "… a better thing's never happened to me. I've reconnected with the band, and found a fantastic person to write with. We've always written well together, Lindsey and I, and this has just spiraled into something really amazing that we've done between us."

On the BBC's *Later…with Jools Holland*, Christine described it as: "an almost Fleetwood Mac record!" Almost, but not quite. Certainly she's very happy to be back with them. "It's that invisible chain, It's that alchemy," she says in *Uncut* magazine. "It's what I want to invest my time and my future in from now on, so I won't leave again."

In the background, of course, still doing their stuff, are John and

MAIN IMAGE

The classic Fleetwood Mac perform on stage at Madison Square Garden, October 2014, New York

Mick, never fully appreciated as a superb rhythm section or as the two most committed and loyal band members, without whom Fleetwood Mac could never have existed.

Now, John, being John, sits quite happily out of the limelight, enjoying his new-found health after a four-year cancer scare, still messing around with boats or relishing the peace and quiet of being at home, reading books or watching his beloved Arsenal FC on Sky Sports.

And Mick? Mick continues to do what he's always done for the last 50 years — raising people's eyebrows but keeping together a great band that should, in reality, have come to a messy end so many times since 1969, when Peter Green walked away. His determination to keep "his baby", Fleetwood Mac, alive and kicking since then has been remarkable and commendable, and long may he continue to do so. But can they really keep on going for much longer?

"Not much longer, for me anyway," said John McVie, in a rare interview, with *Mojo* magazine, in 2015. "It's not the music — it's the peripherals, the travelling. Mick will go on until they put him up against the wall and shoot him. It's sort of worrying… Jesus Christ, will there still be a demand when I'm 75?!"

John McVie is 71. As for Mick, who'll be 70 in 2017, let's put it this way: Fleetwood Mac, he says, is "one hell of a weird, wonderful thing. And if it were a book, you'd want it to end like this."

But not yet, Mick.

In July 2017, Fleetwood Mac appeared at the Classic West festival at the Dodgers Stadium in Los Angeles, followed by the Classic East at Citi Field, New York. Preparations are already underway for a farewell world tour in 2018.

It probably won't be the last...

BIOGRAPHIES

PETER GREEN (GREENBAUM)

BORN: 29 October 1946

PLACE OF BIRTH: Bethnal Green, east London, England

MUSICAL BACKGROUND: Started learning guitar at the age of 10 and was highly influenced by Hank Marvin from the Shadows, American blues guitarists such as Muddy Waters and BB King, and the English composer Vaughan Williams. Joined Bobby Dennis and the Dominos at the age of 15, playing bass guitar. Then joined the Muskrats, followed by the Tridents. Switched to guitar with Peter B's Looners in 1966, where he met Mick Fleetwood. Joined John Mayall's Bluesbreakers three months later. Highly talented and regarded by many as the best British blues guitarist of his generation.

PLAYED ON: [Peter Green's] *Fleetwood Mac, Mr Wonderful, Then Play On*. Minor performances on *Penguin* and *Tusk*

LEFT FLEETWOOD MAC: Made the decision to leave in May 1970 after musical and financial differences with the other band members, but was also suffering from severe mental health issues. He was hospitalised several times during the 1970s.

WHERE IS HE NOW? Lives in London and still performs. Formed the Peter Green Splinter Group in 1996, recording nine albums. Formed his current band, Peter Green and Friends, in 2009.

MICK FLEETWOOD

BORN: 24 June 1947

PLACE OF BIRTH: Redruth, Cornwall, England

MUSICAL BACKGROUND: Struggled at school academically (due to dyslexia) but was bought a drum kit at the age of 13 by his father, Wing Commander John Fleetwood, an RAF fighter pilot and also a drummer. Mick is self-taught and his playing style highly unusual but effective. With his parents' support, left school at 15 and moved to London in an attempt to begin his career as a musician. First band were the Cheynes, who toured with the Rolling Stones.

PLAYED ON: Every Fleetwood Mac album.

LEFT FLEETWOOD MAC: Has never officially left the band.

WHERE IS HE NOW? In-between playing with Fleetwood Mac, Mick has performed on various band members' solo albums and with his own bands — the Mick Fleetwood Band and, more recently, the Mick Fleetwood Blues Band (featuring Rick Vito). Currently lives on the island of Maui in Hawaii, USA, with partner, Chelsea Hill.

JEREMY SPENCER

BORN: 4 July 1948

PLACE OF BIRTH: West Hartlepool, County Durham, England

MUSICAL BACKGROUND: Began piano lessons at the age of nine but took up guitar as a teenager, largely due to his love of the American blues slide guitarist Elmore James, whose influence is obvious throughout his career with Fleetwood Mac. Jeremy was in a band called the Levi Set in 1967 when Decca's record producer, Mike Vernon, introduced him to Peter Green.

PLAYED ON: [Peter Green's] *Fleetwood Mac, Mr Wonderful, Then Play On*

LEFT FLEETWOOD MAC: Left during a US tour in February 1971 in Los Angeles to join a controversial religious cult group, the Children of God. Has been a member (now called the Family International) ever since.

WHERE IS HE NOW? Has continued to play music and formed various bands within the cult organisation, living around the world and playing primarily at religious festivals to promote their work and beliefs. They have also recorded several albums, but with little commercial success. Believed to be currently living in Munich, Germany, with his second wife, Dora.

BOB BRUNNING

BORN: 29 June 1943

PLACE OF BIRTH: Bournemouth, Dorset, England

MUSICAL BACKGROUND: Took up bass guitar in his teens and played in a band in Bournemouth with radio DJ Tony Blackburn. Moved to London in 1964 to study at a teacher training college and played with the college band, Five's Company, who recorded three singles with Pye Records. Peter Green employed him as a temporary bass player in Fleetwood Mac when he responded to an advert in the music newspaper, *Melody Maker,* in July 1967.

PLAYED ON: [Peter Green's] *Fleetwood Mac*

LEFT FLEETWOOD MAC: Joined Fleetwood Mac on the basis that John McVie could reclaim his place if he changed his mind, which he did five months later. Bob left the band in December 1967.

WHERE IS HE NOW? Continued to perform as a bass player with several bands including Savoy Brown, Tramp (with Mick Fleetwood and Danny Kirwan) and his own DeLuxe Blues Band throughout his teaching career. He became headmaster of two south London primary schools and also ran various blues clubs. Wrote several books about the British music scene, including Fleetwood Mac. Bob died aged 68 when he suffered a heart attack at his home in southwest London in October 2011.

JOHN MCVIE

BORN: 26 November 1945

PLACE OF BIRTH: Ealing, west London, England

MUSICAL BACKGROUND: Took up guitar at the age of 14 but soon switched over to bass as no one else wanted to play it. Early influences were Buddy Holly and Jet Harris, bass player for the Shadows. First band was the Krewsaders, formed with other boys from his street in Ealing. Joined John Mayall's Bluesbreakers at the age of 17.

PLAYED ON: Every Fleetwood Mac album.

LEFT FLEETWOOD MAC: Has never officially left the band although did resign on at least one occasion.

WHERE IS HE NOW? When not sailing, John continues to perform with Fleetwood Mac and on various other projects, usually when summoned by best friend, Mick Fleetwood. Currently lives on the island of Maui in Hawaii, USA, with his wife, Julie.

DANNY KIRWAN

BORN: 13 May 1950

PLACE OF BIRTH: Brixton, south London, England
MUSICAL BACKGROUND: Started learning guitar at an early age and was just 17 when discovered by Fleetwood Mac's producer, Mike Vernon, playing in a band called Boilerhouse. Vernon introduced him to Peter Green. Joined Fleetwood Mac in August 1968. Danny's early influences were 1920s big band music, the Shadows' Hank Marvin and jazz guitarist, Django Reinhardt.

PLAYED ON: *Then Play On, Kiln House, Future Games, Bare Trees*

LEFT FLEETWOOD MAC: Sacked in 1972 after an argument backstage with Bob Welch at a US gig turned violent and Kirwan smashed his guitar against a wall and refused to go onstage.

WHERE IS HE NOW? Whereabouts unknown but believed to be living in London after a period of living rough on the streets and in hostels.

BOB WELCH

BORN: 31 August 1945

PLACE OF BIRTH: Los Angeles, California, USA

MUSICAL BACKGROUND: Bob's father, Robert, was a film producer and screenwriter, his mother, Templeton Fox, a singer and actress. Got his first guitar at the age of eight and also learned the clarinet. Early interests were jazz, rhythm and blues, and rock music.

PLAYED ON: *Future Games, Bare Trees, Penguin, Mystery to Me, Heroes Are Hard to Find*

LEFT FLEETWOOD MAC: Resigned from the band in December 1974 because he'd had enough of the constant touring and the internal bickering. He also had marital problems.

WHERE IS HE NOW? Formed the band, Paris, in 1975 and went solo in 1977 as a performer and songwriter, achieving reasonable success. Was managed by Mick Fleetwood and sued Fleetwood Mac in 1994 because of underpaid royalties. The lawsuit was settled in 1996. Some believe this is why he was not invited to the Fleetwood Mac Rock & Roll Hall of Fame induction ceremony in 1998. Sadly, Bob committed suicide aged 67 at his home in Nashville in June 2012 as he was suffering from depression and severe pain following spinal surgery. He left his wife, Wendy, a long suicide note explaining that he did not want to be a burden to her.

CHRISTINE MCVIE (PERFECT)

BORN: 12 July 1943

PLACE OF BIRTH: Bouth, Lancashire (now Cumbria), England

MUSICAL BACKGROUND: Grew up in Smethwick, Birmingham in a musical family — her father, Cyril Perfect, was a concert violinist, her grandfather an organist at Westminster Abbey. Was introduced to the piano at age four but did not study seriously until she was 11. At the age of 15 she became obsessed with rock 'n' roll music when her brother, John, left a Fats Domino songbook on the piano. Also influenced by Sonny Thompson (Freddie King's pianist). Christine is also a talented artist and studied sculpture at college for five years. There she met Stan Webb and Andy Silvester, who formed Chicken Shack in 1967. Left Chicken Shack after working as a session piano player for Fleetwood Mac on three albums before joining them officially in 1970.

PLAYED ON: Every Fleetwood Mac album except [Peter Green's] *Fleetwood Mac.*

LEFT FLEETWOOD MAC: Christine was inducted into the Rock & Roll Hall of Fame and received the Brit Award for Outstanding Contribution to Music in 1998, but at that time had developed a fear of flying and left the band to live in semi-retirement for the next 16 years near Canterbury in Kent.

WHERE IS SHE NOW? Returned to the stage with Fleetwood Mac at London's O2 Arena in September 2013, and re-joine d the band officially in January 2014. Currently lives in London and, in June 2017, released a new album with Lindsey: *Lindsey Buckingham/Christine McVie.*

BOB WESTON

BORN: 1 November 1947

PLACE OF BIRTH: Plymouth, Devon, England

MUSICAL BACKGROUND: Began lessons on the violin at the age of eight, but switched to guitar at 12. Main influences were Muddy Waters, Howlin' Wolf's guitarist Hubert Sumlin, and jazz guitarist Django Reinhardt. Moved to London in the mid-'60s and joined the Kinetic, a British band that worked mainly in France, where they supported the likes of Jimi Hendrix and Chuck Berry. In 1970, he joined Long John Baldry's band.

PLAYED ON: *Penguin, Mystery to Me*

LEFT FLEETWOOD MAC: Was sacked by the band in 1973 when it was revealed he had been having an affair with Mick Fleetwood's wife, Jenny.

WHERE IS HE NOW? Went on to record three solo albums and played with various other performers including Dana Gillespie, Murray Head, Sandy Denny, Bob Welch and Danny Kirwan. Bob died aged 64 at his flat in Brent Cross, north London in January 2012 as the result of a gastrointestinal haemorrhage and cirrhosis of the liver.

DAVE WALKER

BORN: 25 January 1945

PLACE OF BIRTH: Walsall, West Midlands, England

MUSICAL BACKGROUND: Influenced by singers such as Paul Robeson, Hoagy Carmichael and Sister Rosetta Tharpe, Dave started singing at a local Methodist church in Walsall at a very early age, being raised by his strict and religious grandmother. His father, who was in the US Airforce, was killed in the last months of World War II. Dave never met him. First band was the Redcaps, who supported the Beatles four times. Joined a band called Beckett followed by the Idle Race when Jeff Lynne and Roy Wood left to form the Move. Went on to play with Savoy Brown from 1971-72, before joining Fleetwood Mac in August '72.

PLAYED ON: *Penguin*

LEFT FLEETWOOD MAC: Was sacked in 1973 when it was felt his vocal style and overpowering stage performance were not appropriate.

WHERE IS HE NOW? Went on to play for various other bands including Black Sabbath, Savoy Brown and his own Dave Walker Band. Since then he has recorded with psychedelic revivalists Donovan's Brain and singer Angie Pepper, before releasing a critically acclaimed solo album *Walking Underwater* in 2007. Currently lives in Bozeman, Montana, USA.

LINDSEY BUCKINGHAM

BORN: 3 October 1949

PLACE OF BIRTH: Palo Alto, California, USA

MUSICAL BACKGROUND: Began playing a toy Mickey Mouse guitar when just seven years old but his parents recognised his talent and bought him a Harmony guitar. Taught himself to play. By the age of 13 he was largely influenced by American folk music and banjo-style finger picking, particularly the Kingston Trio from San Francisco Bay. In 1966, aged 17, joined a San Francisco band called Fritz as bass player and vocalist. His school friend, Stevie Nicks, joined the band as second vocalist shortly afterwards.

PLAYED ON: *Fleetwood Mac, Rumours, Tusk, Live, Mirage, Tango in the Night, Behind the Mask* (acoustic guitar on title track), *Time* (backing vocals on 'Nothing Without You'), *The Dance, Say You Will*

LEFT FLEETWOOD MAC: Left the band in August 1987 to concentrate on solo work but returned for the recording and tour of *The Dance* in May 1997 and has officially been with them since.

WHERE IS HE NOW? Lives in Los Angeles with his wife, Kristen Messner, and their three children. Since 2003, when Fleetwood Mac's *Say You Will* was released, he has recorded four studio and two live solo albums. In June 2017 he released a new album with Christine: *Lindsey Buckingham/Christine McVie*.

STEVIE NICKS

BORN: 26 May 1948

PLACE OF BIRTH: Phoenix, Arizona, USA

MUSICAL BACKGROUND: Influenced by her grandfather, Aaron Nicks, a country singer who encouraged her to accompany him from the age of around four years old. First band were the Changing Times at high school in Los Angeles. When her parents moved to San Francisco, she met Lindsey Buckingham at a school church meeting and they sang together for the first time. Joined Lindsey's band Fritz in 1966.

PLAYED ON: *Fleetwood Mac, Rumours, Tusk, Live, Mirage, Tango in the Night, Behind the Mask, The Dance, Say You Will*

LEFT FLEETWOOD MAC: Following a disagreement with Mick Fleetwood concerning his refusal to allow her song 'Silver Springs' to be used on her album, *Timespace: The Best of Stevie Nicks*, she left the band in 1991 to concentrate on her solo career. Returned for the recording and tour of *The Dance* in May 1997 and has officially been with them since.

WHERE IS SHE NOW? Since 2003 Stevie has released two more solo studio and one live album, and toured regularly both solo and with other performers. She lives in Los Angeles.

BILLY BURNETTE

BORN: 8 May 1953

PLACE OF BIRTH: Memphis, Tennessee, USA

MUSICAL BACKGROUND: From a very musical family. His father, Dorsey, and uncle, Johnny, were both members of the 1950s rockabilly group, the Rock and Roll Trio, and wrote songs for Ricky Nelson. Billy appeared on one of Ricky's hit singles at just seven years of age. Taught himself to play guitar and toured with Brenda Lee aged just 13. Began writing songs at around 15 or 16 and released his first solo album when just 18 years old.

PLAYED ON: *Behind the Mask, Time*

LEFT FLEETWOOD MAC: Left after the *Behind the Mask* tour in November 1991 to concentrate on a solo career, but re-joined them in 1994 to record *Time*. Left the band again towards the end of 1995 after the disappointing *Time* tour and formed a country duo with Bekka Bramlett.

WHERE IS HE NOW? Since leaving Fleetwood Mac, Billy has recorded five more solo albums and in the last few years toured with Bob Dylan and Creedence Clearwater Revival's John Fogerty, as well as with Mick Fleetwood's Zoo. Currently lives in Nashville, Tennessee.

RICK VITO

BORN: 13 October 1949

PLACE OF BIRTH: Philadelphia, Pennsylvania, USA

MUSICAL BACKGROUND: Early influences were Jerry Lee Lewis, Fats Domino Little Richard and, from the age of around six years old, Elvis Presley, who he would imitate with his mother's acoustic guitar. Started guitar lessons soon after but decided to give up and teach himself, inspired by Jerry Cole, session guitarist who played with just about everyone, and slide guitar maestro Elmore James. Peter Green was also a major influence, both on guitar and vocally. First live performance was at the age of 14 with friends at a local teen dance. Went on to play with Bob Seger, Rita Coolidge, Jackson Browne, Dolly Parton, Todd Rundgren, John Mayall, Roy Orbison and many others.

PLAYED ON: *Behind the Mask*

LEFT FLEETWOOD MAC: Left in November 1991 after recording *Behind the Mask* to work with Stevie Nicks on her record label, Modern Records, and produce his first solo album, *King of Hearts*.

WHERE IS HE NOW? Has continued to perform as a much in-demand session and touring guitarist for many big names, as well as recording seven solo albums. Currently lives between Nashville, Tennessee and Makawao, Hawaii, USA.

BEKKA BRAMLETT

BORN: 19 April 1968

PLACE OF BIRTH: Los Angeles, California, USA

MUSICAL BACKGROUND: Daughter of Delaney and Bonnie Bramlett, a successful American duo who fronted an R'n'B ensemble, 'Delaney & Bonnie and Friends', which included Duane Allman, Gregg Allman, George Harrison, Leon Russell, Bobby Whitlock, Dave Mason, Rita Coolidge and Eric Clapton. In 1991-92 Bekka appeared with Mick Fleetwood's Zoo and appeared on the album *Shakin' the Cage*.

PLAYED ON: *Time*

LEFT FLEETWOOD MAC: Following a tour to promote *Time*, she left with Billy Burnette towards the end of 1995 to form a new duo, 'Bekka & Billy'.

WHERE IS SHE NOW? Recorded an album with Billy Burnette and two solo albums. Has worked as a backing singer for a variety of performers including Belinda Carlisle, Joe Cocker, Kenny Rogers, Rita Coolidge, Etta James, Robert Plant, Buddy Guy, Bonnie Tyler and Albert Lee. Currently lives in Nashville, Tennessee, USA.

DAVE MASON

BORN: 10 May 1946

PLACE OF BIRTH: Worcester, Worcestershire, England

MUSICAL BACKGROUND: Began playing guitar at the age of 16 and was a professional musician by 17 in his first band, the Jaguars. Met Jim Capaldi in his next band, the Hellions. Formed the Deep Feeling with Capaldi before meeting Steve Winwood and Chris Wood to form one of the UK's most influential bands, Traffic. Wrote their second Top 5 hit, 'Hole in My Shoe' which got to No. 2. Played on various famous albums with the likes of Paul McCartney, George Harrison, Jimi Hendrix and the Rolling Stones and was one of several famous musicians to join 'Delaney & Bonnie and Friends'.

PLAYED ON: *Time*

LEFT FLEETWOOD MAC: Following a tour to promote *Time*, Dave returned to session and solo work towards the end of 1995.

WHERE IS HE NOW? Continues to perform both solo and with his band Traffic Jam. Supports several charitable organisations including Little Kids Rock, which provides free musical education for US children. Currently lives in Carson City, Nevada, USA.

STUDIO ALBUMS

[PETER GREEN'S] FLEETWOOD MAC

1968

PRODUCER: Mike Vernon
RECORDED: CBS Studios, London
UK: No.4
USA: Did not chart

Fleetwood Mac's eponymous debut LP (sometimes referred to as [Peter Green's] *Fleetwood Mac*, or the 'Dog and Dustbin' LP) was one of the best albums to appear from the British blues explosion amongst a crowded genre inhabited by the likes of the Rolling Stones, John Mayall's Bluesbreakers, Cream, the Groundhogs, Savoy Brown, Ten Years After, Chicken Shack et al.

Peter Green's guitar playing is exceptional on his own blues songs, jumbled in among some classic numbers, while Fleetwood Mac's other guitarist, the diminutive Jeremy Spencer, is clearly influenced by the best slide guitarist of the post-war period, Elmore James ('Shake Your Moneymaker' and 'Got to Move' being fine examples). There's no doubt that, as would be the case on all of Fleetwood Mac's albums featuring Peter Green, his guitar and harmonica playing, lead vocals and songwriting skills (take a listen to the superb 'The World Keep on Turning') outshone just about everyone else in the UK at that stage — including the likes of Eric Clapton, Jeff Beck and Jimmy Page.

On tracks such as 'Looking for Somebody' and 'Long Grey Mare' (one of the few recordings with Bob Brunning on bass) and 'I Loved Another Woman', Peter Green (with the backing of solid rhythms laid down by Mick Fleetwood and John McVie) offered glimpses of what was just around the corner.

Certainly, at that stage, those talents were recognised by the British press ("Committed blues … Highly recommended," said *Melody Maker*) and the British public who, to everyone's surprise, launched Fleetwood Mac's debut album to No. 4 in the UK charts. For blues fans, this is simply a great album, but for those who have only ever experienced the Lindsey Buckingham/Stevie Nicks era, nothing here bears any resemblance to what was to come. Certainly worth a listen for those curious as to where the roots of Fleetwood Mac were planted 10 years earlier.

MR WONDERFUL

1968

PRODUCER: Mike Vernon
RECORDED: CBS Studios, London
UK: No. 10
USA: Did not chart

Fleetwood Mac's second album, *Mr Wonderful*, was generally considered something of a disappointment compared to their successful debut, despite reaching No. 10 in the UK charts and being their first LP to feature (uncredited) a session from Chicken Shack's keyboardist, Christine Perfect — soon to be John McVie's wife.

The album's not terrible but does suffer from several weaknesses. First, it was recorded as simply as possible as a live show in the studio, with few recording elaborations. If it was an attempt to capture a live performance, it succeeds only if the listener has bought a cheap ticket some distance from the stage on a windy day. Vocals, drums and guitars all sound distant and slightly muffled.

Jeremy Spencer's obsession with Elmore James's slide guitar work results in four of the songs being almost identical 12-bar shuffles with the same opening riff. Peter Green's songs once again are stronger, especially the opener 'Stop Messin' Round' and the slow blues 'Love That Burns', both of which would find their way onto Fleetwood Mac's first *Greatest Hits* album in 1971. For some reason, probably legal issues, all of Peter Green's songs on *Mr Wonderful* are co-credited with someone by the name of C.G. Adams — in fact the stage name of Fleetwood Mac's manager, Clifford Davis, who was also a songwriter and musician.

RIGHT

[Peter Green's] *Fleetwood Mac* cover

As for the cover … it has to be seen to be believed. The lanky, crazed-looking Mick Fleetwood, naked, behind some greenery, holding a spooky doll and toy dog. Nothing too wonderful about that, either, but probably more memorable than most of the songs.

THEN PLAY ON

1969

PRODUCER: Fleetwood Mac
RECORDED: De Lane Lea Studios, London
UK: No. 6
USA: No. 109

Somewhere between Fleetwood Mac's first two blues-based LPs and their soft-rock/pop output with Lindsey and Stevie from 1975, you'll find this superb album that manages to merge blues, soft-rock, hard-rock, folk, pop, easy listening, jazz and even a bit of early psychedelic prog, influencing just about everything else that was to come. How could it not? Nothing had been left out.

During the short period between *Mr Wonderful* and this, their third studio album, *Then Play On* (the title misquoting Shakespeare's line from *Twelfth Night*: "If music be the food of love, play on,") several important events had taken place that would dramatically affect the next 50 years for Fleetwood Mac; some good, some not so good.

First, although still credited as a member of the band, Jeremy Spencer contributed very little, if anything, to this LP due to his disillusionment at Peter Green's refusal to include more Elmore James slide guitar-based songs. In his place arrived the talented 18-year-old Danny Kirwan, an excellent south London guitarist, singer and songwriter whose broad palette of sounds would have a considerable impact over the next four years. Christine Perfect once again added some top drawer keyboard playing but was not credited due to contract issues.

There were no less than seven Kirwan songs on this, his first Mac LP, among them 'My Dream', a rather morose but beautiful instrumental, and 'Although the Sun Is Shining', a lovely folk song drawing comparisons with Nick Drake and which could easily have appeared

on Mac's first LP with Lindsey Buckingham and Stevie Nicks a few years later.

By the time this LP was recorded, Fleetwood Mac had toured America for the first time and been clearly influenced by the Grateful Dead and the Band. Green's songs were still blues-tinged but dripping with genuine sadness. Beautiful melodies captured from the same song-pool as their recent No. 1 hit, 'Albatross', were used to express Green's tragic lyrics: "Someday I'll die and maybe then I'll be with you," from 'Closing My Eyes'; "Do you really give a damn for me?" from 'Showbiz Blues'; here was a brilliant musician living a deeply troubled life.

But the twin guitar work between Green and Kirwan on the two jam tracks 'Searching for Madge' and the similar African beats of 'Fighting for Madge' (strangely listing John McVie and Mick Fleetwood respectively as the composers), plus the album's opening song, 'Coming Your Way', demonstrated the strong bond Green and Kirwan were enjoying and developing almost immediately. Their musical relationship boded well on what was undoubtedly the best but proved, sadly, also to be the last LP of Fleetwood Mac's Peter Green era. Apart from a couple of uncredited performance on *Penguin* and *Tusk*, his Mac days were over. But who knows? "If music be the food of love …"

KILN HOUSE

1970

PRODUCER: Fleetwood Mac
RECORDED: De Lane Lea Studios, London and Rolling Stones Mobile Studio, Benifold, Alton
UK: No. 39
USA: No. 69

With Peter Green having left the building it was ironic that Fleetwood Mac's next LP a year later would kick off with an obvious parody of Elvis Presley on Jeremy Spencer's 'This is the Rock'. An unusual opener but a bit of fun … until you realise Spencer has no less than three more parodies (the likes of Fats Waller, Buddy Holly and Johnny Cash) spread across the LP's two sides. There is a limit to how much 'fun' a musical parody can provide; certainly Mr Green would not have been amused.

Apart from those Spencer contributions, the remaining four members (plus Christine McVie — now John's wife — providing excellent but uncredited keyboards once again) continued to broaden the band's musical experimentation and influences in the absence of Peter's leadership. Christine also provided the delightful cover artwork for *Kiln House*, reminding everyone that she's also a talented artist.

Danny Kirwan showcased two excellent numbers with 'Jewel Eyed Judy', sounding uncannily like an unknown remnant from the Beatles' White Album; while 'Earl Gray' could well be a TV theme tune from a 70s romantic comedy. Furthermore, despite seeming unlikely, he and Spencer were gelling well on the band's new twin guitar duets. 'Station Man' could be Delaney and Bonnie jamming with Steve Stills on the West Coast; and on the hard-rocking 'Tell Me All the Things You Do', just close your eyes and you're rocking along to Humble Pie.

'One Together' revealed new vocal harmony skills no one had expected (thanks to Christine's contribution), while the album concluded with the folky, also Beatles-influenced, 'Mission Bell', which seemed to suggest this might be the direction in which the band might be heading. But then play the curious *Kiln House* a couple more times and the question raises its head: where, exactly? The Beatles? The Stones? The Band? The Rubettes? Did anyone really have any idea?

FUTURE GAMES

1971

PRODUCER: Fleetwood Mac
RECORDED: Advision Sound Studios, London
UK: Did not chart
USA: No. 91

Recorded at Advision Studios in London, this was Fleetwood Mac's fifth studio LP, by which time Jeremy Spencer had found God and been replaced by Bob Welch; Christine McVie had begun to

contribute and sing more songs; and the band had sort of found the sort of direction in which they sort of wanted to head.

Born and raised in Los Angeles, Bob Welch had been recommended to them by an American friend who knew that he happened to be living in Paris at the time and was looking for work— the first American musician to join Fleetwood Mac. Mick loved Bob's cool, California vocals and guitar style and, with the bonus of songwriting skills, he was exactly what they needed to recover from losing Peter Green and Jeremy Spencer so suddenly. It was also a clear indication that the band were looking to move away from the blues towards more ethereal, folky West Coast sounds.

Take a listen to Christine McVie's first ever Fleetwood Mac song, 'Morning Rain', second track, side one, and suddenly you're listening to the Fleetwood Mac we now all know: American soft rock guitars, strong piano rhythms, and Crosby, Stills & Nash style close harmonies — including Welch's suggestion to mix male and female voices.

Although Bob Welch only contributed two songs to *Future Games*, his eight-minute title track that closes side one is superb, with a haunting melody and excellent lead guitar from Danny Kirwan, whose own opener 'Woman of a Thousand Years' kicks off with his signature guitar sound. In fact, everything on side one is pretty good — even the short filler 'What a Shame' featuring Christine's McVie's brother, John Perfect, on saxophone; a little jam that ends too soon.

On side two, Christine's 'Show Me a Smile' is among her loveliest ever ballads and a great vocal performance, while Kirwan's 'Sands of Time' is the perfect continuation of those classic '70s guitar sounds. Regardless of two excellent guitar players, however, there's no doubt that it's the combined talents and components of Fleetwood/McVie/McVie that are Fleetwood Mac's real future games.

There's not really a bad track on this album; it may be a mishmash of styles but it's also the first step towards superstardom. It was definitely undervalued by the public and media at the time — still is today — but you can understand why it didn't chart in the UK and only just made it into the USA's *Billboard* Hot 100. As Nick Logan commented in *New Musical Express*: "…a set that is more a foundation for the growth of a new band than the sum total and end product of their individual potential."

BARE TREES

1972

PRODUCER: Fleetwood Mac
RECORDED: De Lane Lea Studios, London
UK: Did not chart
USA: No. 70

Bare Trees resumed where *Future Games* had finished the previous year with another fine collection of laid back '70s songwriter sounds, continuing the journey towards the new Fleetwood Mac (almost) throughout. This was more obviously a transition LP that gelled the band (rather than individual talent) more coherently (particularly Danny Kirwan and Bob Welch's twin guitar work) than *Future Games* achieved, but then tails off a little towards the end.

There's no doubt that Danny Kirwan is the focal point of this LP, writing five songs compared to Christine McVie and Bob Welch's two each. Danny's 'Child of Mine' kicks off the LP very nicely, with some great rhythm work from Mick and John, again signalling that distinctive Fleetwood Mac drums and bass sound. 'Sunny Side of Heaven' is equally impressive — what other bands since the Shadows were playing similar instrumentals in the '70s? Perfect theme music.

Christine McVie's 'Spare Me a Little of Your Love' was arguably her best song to date and well on the way to defining that unique Fleetwood Mac sound just three years down the road. Ironically, her other song on *Bare Trees*, 'Homeward Bound' foretells almost three decades of life on the road with Fleetwood Mac, but not at a level of intensity she could ever have envisaged.

Bob Welch's 'Sentimental Lady' on side two went on to become his first solo hit record when re-recorded in 1977, although most would agree Fleetwood Mac's version is much better: excellent vocal harmonies with Christine, impressive guitar solos from Welch and Kirwan, and a definite move towards West Coast soft rock. His earlier contribution, 'The Ghost', is impressively California sunshine pop considering it's for an album revolving around the theme of an English grey, bleak, mid-winter (John McVie's photograph of bare trees adorning the front cover).

To me, that's where *Bare Trees* ultimately loses its way. Danny Kirwan's 'Dust' based on a Rupert Brooke poem segues into 'Thoughts on a Grey Day', a poem written and read by a 68 year-old neighbour of the band, Aileen Scarrott, on the beauty of winter landscapes. Worthy, but…

Whatever, *Bare Trees* eventually (by the late '80s) sold over a million copies and attained platinum status. Overall, another misunderstood but likeable LP.

PENGUIN

1973

PRODUCER: Fleetwood Mac and Martin Birch
RECORDED: Rolling Stones Mobile Studio, Benifold, Alton
UK: Did not chart
USA: No. 49

Why *Penguin*? Because John McVie was a member of the Zoological Society and had a bit of a thing about these cute little aquatic, flightless birds. He would often visit London Zoo to photograph them (also explaining, up to a point, why his bio picture on the back cover of *Future Games* was actually one of a penguin…)

More importantly, this was the first Fleetwood Mac LP since the sudden departure of Danny Kirwan, replaced by new band members Bob Weston from Plymouth — a very capable slide guitarist — and singer/harmonica player Dave Walker — a well-respected musician from Walsall who had performed with Idle Race and Savoy Brown and later went on to join Black Sabbath for a brief period.

From the very first three numbers — Christine McVie's 'Remember Me', Bob Welch's 'Bright Fire' and Christine's 'Dissatisfied' — it's obvious these are the dominant force in this new Fleetwood Mac line-up. Christine's brace of songs clearly identify her promotion within the band — two good numbers but both on the subject of troubled relationships. In between comes Bob Welch's equally impressive West Coast 'Bright Fire', with its lovely melody and nice guitar.

Three tracks in and you begin to think, this is a pretty good album… and then comes a cover of Holland-Dozier-Holland's 1966 hit for Jr. Walker & the All Stars, '(I'm a) Road Runner'. It's a decent cover, but why choose it? Just to give Dave Walker something to justify his inclusion? Was he related to Jr.?

Side two kicks off with Dave Walker's only composition, 'The Derelict' — a country blues ballad that sounds much like the Band and isn't bad at all, with nice banjo and harmonica from Bob Weston, but neither the song or Walker's voice are Fleetwood Mac. It's one of those pleasant little fillers that starts off slowly and then peters out altogether.

Next up, however, is *Penguin*'s highlight — 'Revelation' — written and largely performed by Bob Welch but a song that could so easily have been written and performed by Peter Green. Top drumming from Mick and a great guitar and bass workout from Bob Welch (purportedly because John McVie was out on a drinking bender with Dave Walker).

The remaining three tracks are not of the same quality as 'Revelation', although the best of them, Bob Welch's 'Night Watch' actually features Peter Green (uncredited) playing some great guitar, but so far back in the mix that it could easily be missed altogether. Which kind of sums up the album, sadly.

Commented *Melody Maker*: "*Penguin* is a wishy-washy affair

without soul or direction." A little harsh; this was Fleetwood Mac's first US Top 50 LP and is not terrible, but neither is it great, offering too many fillers from a band that had not yet had a chance to gel. Too much gelling and un-gelling in certain other ways, however, revealed that the first cracks in Fleetwood Mac's yet another new façade were beginning to show.

MYSTERY TO ME

1973

PRODUCER: Fleetwood Mac and Martin Birch
RECORDED: Rolling Stones Mobile Studio, Benifold, Alton
UK: Did not chart
USA: No. 67

Despite struggling to find enough decent material to make *Penguin* a great LP, Fleetwood Mac were back in the Rolling Stones mobile studio at Benifold within a few months to record their eighth studio LP, *Mystery to Me*. A good title in terms of why they felt the need to do so; what did they hope to achieve so quickly?

Soon after recording began Dave Walker was sacked by the band simply because he didn't fit in and was starting to dominate live performances. Instead, this was an opportunity for Bob Welch to dominate Fleetwood Mac. Of the 12 songs on this LP, Welch had written six by himself and one with Christine McVie. Christine had written another four, leaving yet another unexpected cover of future 10cc member Graham Gouldman's hit song 'For Your Love', which been a hit for the Yardbirds in 1965.

The opener, the laid-back 'Emerald Eyes', was another Crosby, Stills & Nash soundalike with Welch's spacey lyrics and great backup vocals from Christine McVie. Two of Christine's songs 'Believe Me' and 'Just Crazy Love' followed — decent soft-rock numbers once again (surprise, surprise) about troubled relationships, but not her best.

Welch's jazzy and lyrically interesting 'Hypnotized' (based on paranormal activities), sounding remarkably like Steely Dan, is a very good song, as is his last number on side one, the funky 'Keep on Going' — unusually sung not by the composer but Christine McVie, who does a great job. Between them comes an interesting reggae number credited to Bob Weston, John McVie and Bob Welch.

Welch's equally funky 'The City', 'Miles Away' and 'Somebody' kick off side two and are all decent songs but few would recognise them as Fleetwood Mac numbers if they didn't know any better. Again, so far, a decent album but one that lacks any focus; once again the question raises its head — where is this band going?

The answer lies in two of the album's last three numbers, both being examples of Christine McVie's songwriting brilliance beginning to shine through. Sadly, both are influenced by the personal heartbreak she and John were experiencing at the time. First, 'The Way I Feel' sounds suspiciously like a love letter to the band's recording engineer, Martin Birch, with who Christine was having an affair at the time.

And if we then ignore the cover of 'For Your Love' (other than to ask "why?"), we can quickly move on to the final track, which, ironically, is called 'Why' — undoubtedly the best song on the record and the strongest indication of what Christine was capable of. Getting underway with a one-minute slide guitar blues solo from Bob Weston, Christine then offers a sad end-of-love letter: "There's no use in crying, it's all over, but I know there'll always be another day…"

With a beautiful string arrangement from Richard Hewson, it's a song that gets better each time you hear it.

So Christine's marriage to John is as good as over. It also becomes apparent that Mick Fleetwood's wife Jenny is having an affair with Bob Weston. The other question everyone wants an answer to is: How on earth did Fleetwood Mac keep things together sufficiently to record *Mystery to Me* and go on tour with it? It's a mystery to just about everybody. And there's worse to come.

HEROES ARE HARD TO FIND

1974

PRODUCER: Fleetwood Mac and Bob Hughes
RECORDED: Angel City Sound, Los Angeles
UK: Did not chart
USA: No. 34

Bob Weston had to go, for obvious reasons. And, tired of the stress and strain resulting from touring and recording with Fleetwood Mac for three and a half years, this also proved to be Bob Welch's last album with the band, contributing seven songs. The more you hear of Bob Welch, the more you realise what an excellent songwriter and performer he could be; his contribution to Fleetwood Mac has often been undervalued.

With an additional four songs from Christine McVie, she and Welch worked together as a cohesive force to produce one of their most diverse albums. Recorded in Los Angeles, it perfectly suited the US AOR [adult-oriented rock] market at that time (reaching No. 34 in the US, their highest to date) but once again failed to chart in the UK.

Christine's 'Heroes Are Hard to Find' got the album off to a great start with a nice R'n'B number including a full brass section. Welch then brings three numbers to the table — the jazzy 'Coming Home' followed by the Peter Green-influenced 'Angel', and then another paean to the paranormal with 'Bermuda Triangle', which almost, with some syrupy strings, could have stumbled into Barry Manilow territory.

Then we make the first journey into country music with Christine's excellent 'Come a Little Bit Closer' featuring superb pedal steel guitar from the Flying Burrito Brothers' Sneaky Pete Kleinow. Continuing the theme, the side two opener by Bob Welch, 'She's Changing Me', offers some great Eagles-like harmonies from he and Christine.

This LP can truly boast a great first half and equally good start to side two but then runs out of steam. Christine's 'Bad Loser' (another Peter Green-influenced song with solid rhythm work

RIGHT

Contact sheet of Fleetwood Mac in Sound City studios, Los Angeles, February 1975, recording *Fleetwood Mac*

from Mick Fleetwood and John McVie) is about as good as the rest of it gets, which is a shame. Welch's remaining three numbers make a move towards Steve Miller-sounding AOR soft rock or, with the closing number 'Safe Harbour', offers little more than rather weak 'Albatross' guitar noodling. Only Christine's final contribution 'Prove Your Love' is worth a second listen.

Interesting, yes, diverse, yes, enjoyable, yes, and potentially a great album, but not quite there, and often just forgotten. *Heroes Are Hard to Find* was certainly a step in the right direction, but something bigger and better was just around the corner…

FLEETWOOD MAC

1975

PRODUCER: Fleetwood Mac and Keith Olsen
RECORDED: Sound City, Los Angeles
UK: No. 23
USA: No. 1

This was Fleetwood Mac's 10th studio and second eponymous LP, often referred to as the 'White Album' to distinguish it from their debut release, and the first without Bob Welch for almost four years. Apart from contributing several excellent songs to Fleetwood Mac's playlist, and persuading the band to move to happier climes in Los Angeles, Welch had also introduced the band to '70s AOR soft rock and the financial success it can bring, so when he upped and left in December 1974, Mick Fleetwood knew exactly what he needed to replace him, and where to find them.

It was a brilliant piece of A and R [artists and repertoire] management by Mick to recruit Lindsey Buckingham and Stevie Nicks from Sound City and bring about the rebirth of Fleetwood Mac. Many claim that it was only when the Californian duo came on board that Fleetwood Mac became a West Coast pop band, transforming its sound and identity and persuading Christine McVie to join their soft rock gang.

Truth is, if you listen to their previous five LPs, Bob Welch's contribution to that sound should not be underestimated, and Christine's songwriting skills had already developed by leaps and bounds.

The risk already identified, however, was that the band were becoming rather too mellow and laid back. What Buckingham did — just listen to his opener on *Fleetwood Mac*, 'Monday Morning' — was to raise the bar with new, edgy songs and raw, finger-flicking, Les Paul guitar-playing, which pretty much set the tone and standard for the next few years. "They've decided to abandon the guitar hero syndrome [for] the (lucrative) mainstream of soft pop-rock," said Roy Carr in *New Musical Express*. How wrong, but also how right, he was.

After Buckingham's opener he takes a back seat, contributing only the final song 'I'm So Afraid', and one co-written with Christine, 'World Turning'; the rest, apart from the virtually ubiquitous Fleetwood Mac cover (another Eagles-ish 'Blue Letter' written by Lindsey and Stevie's friends Michael and Richard Curtis), is handed over to the girls. And what a job they do: Stevie Nicks's brilliant 'Rhiannon' and Christine's memorable 'Say You Love Me' and 'Over My Head' all became Top 20 hit singles in the USA, while the LP climbed to No. 1.

Equally impressive are Stevie's beautiful 'Landslide' and Lindsey/Christine's 'World Turning'. In fact, there are no bad songs or fillers (except possibly Christine's 'Sugar Daddy', which does sound remarkably like an extra verse of 'Say You Love Me'). The 'White Album' was, in effect, a blank canvas for these five great, individual musicians to meld together and create something much stronger than the sum of their individual talents — a blueprint for the future of Fleetwood Mac.

And if they were this good, creating and recording an album so impressive within six months of meeting one another, what would they be capable of with a bit more time? Two years later we would find out.

RIGHT

John McVie in Sound City studios, Los Angeles, 1975

RUMOURS

1977

PRODUCER: Fleetwood Mac, Ken Caillat and Richard Dashut
RECORDED: Record Plant, Sausalito and Los Angeles;
Wally Heider Recording, Los Angeles; Criteria Recording
Studios, Miami; Davlen Sound Studios, Hollywood; Zellerbach
Auditorium, Berkeley, California
UK: No. 1
USA: No. 1

Where does one begin writing a review of *Rumours* when
it's all been said so many times before? Or without using the
word 'perfect'? Not easy. Let's leave it to Mick Fleetwood who
described *Rumours* as "the most important album we ever
made", because it provided them with the power and the cash
to continue making records for years to come, despite their
careers being on the rocks more than once. That's more of a
professional musician's view of *Rumours*. Making a living is far
more important than winning awards.

Based on the last count, with various reissues and remasters
being released on a regular basis, *Rumours* has now sold more
than 40million copies and counting. Its enduring quality cannot
be questioned. Take a look at just about any Top 50 albums
of all time lists, and it will be up there somewhere among the
likes of Pink Floyd's *Dark Side of the Moon*, the Beatles' *Sgt.
Pepper's Lonely Hearts Club Band* and Michael Jackson's
Thriller.

Back in 1977 it achieved the highest pre-orders for an LP ever —
800,000 copies — and sold over 10million copies within a year.

Did anyone not like it? In truth, *Rumours* wasn't that well-
received by everyone when it was launched. Punk and new
wave reached their peak in 1977 and it wasn't cool to admit
you liked an album produced by a bunch of boring old farts like
Fleetwood Mac.

That year, the Clash released their first eponymous LP, the
Sex Pistols' *Never Mind the Bollocks*, the Ramones' *Rocket to
Russia*, Elvis Costello's *My Aim is True*, Ian Dury's *New Boots
and Panties!!*, Iggy Pop's *Lust For Life* … these were so much
cooler than Fleetwood Mac! Now, 50 years later, people who
wore bin liners and bondage gear back in 1977 will often admit
that *Rumours* was one of their guilty pleasures.

So why is it so good? Everything about *Rumours*, from the
cover artwork to the songs and the running order, is flawless.
Up there on the high pedestal it shares with the Beatles' and
Pink Floyd's masterpieces, this is one of those albums that
should be played from start to finish to really appreciate its
brilliance. From Lindsey Buckingham's opener 'Second Hand
News' (about his break-up with Stevie Nicks) through to her
closing 'Gold Dust Woman' (about her cocaine addiction), every
track conveys the drama of personal turmoil unlike any other
album.

Against a background of broken hearts, booze and drug
addictions, three of the main characters not only manage to
be in the same room together and perform but harmonise
beautifully; listen to 'The Chain'. Add John McVie's emotive
bassline (the theme to TV's Formula 1 motor racing) to hear
perfection, credited to all five of them. Lindsey Buckingham's
'Go Your Own Way' is an undisguised poison pen letter to
Stevie — "Shacking up is all you want to do"; her reply was
'Dreams' — "listen carefully to the sound of your loneliness".

Now listen to Christine McVie's four tracks — all based on
relationships. The first, 'Don't Stop', is reassurance for husband,
John, that everything's going to be ok, while 'You Make Loving
Fun' celebrates her new relationship with the band's lighting
director. In the middle sits Mick Fleetwood trying to prevent
pistols at dawn.

As John McVie said, "I'd be sitting there in the studio while they
were mixing 'Don't Stop', and I'd listen to the words which were
mostly about me, and I'd get a lump in my throat. I'd turn around
and the writer's sitting right there."

Recording *Rumours* wasn't easy for any of them, but worth all
the pain.

RIGHT

Backstage at Wembley Arena, London, 1980, with just a few of
their UK sales awards for Rumours and Tusk

TUSK

1979

PRODUCER: Fleetwood Mac, Ken Caillat and Richard Dashut
RECORDED: The Village Recorder, Studio D and Lindsey
Buckingham's home studio
UK: No. 1
USA: No. 4

Fleetwood Mac knew they'd never top *Rumours*, whatever Warner
Bros were hoping for as they handed over a blank cheque. Instead of
following the path of least resistance, Lindsey Buckingham — inspired
by the Clash and Talking Heads — decided to follow his new wave
instincts and create a sprawling, manic and, at times, totally incoherent
20-track double album. Lindsey said he wanted to "shake people up and
make them think". He certainly achieved that much. With the Warner
Bros execs loosening their ties in horror as they listened to it for the first
time and checked their bank statements, *Tusk* would be considered a
total flop, even though it went on to sell around 5million copies.

There aren't many other albums like this — three very different
songwriters and performers all in the same band heading in three
equally different directions across myriad styles... Ring any bells?
The Beatles' double album *The Beatles* (or White Album) was the
first of its kind, the band's attempt to create something in complete
contrast to the hugely successful *Sgt. Pepper's Lonely Hearts Club
Band*. Creative differences led to big fall-outs, which resulted in an
LP regarded by some fans and critics at the time as a complete
mess. Now it's considered one of the greatest albums of all time.

After eight years of unprecedented success, the Beatles could get
away with it, but could Lindsey Buckingham and Fleetwood Mac?
As Mick Fleetwood said to him: "Thanks for ruining our career." He
now claims it's his second favourite Fleetwood Mac LP.

Using weird recording techniques such as hitting tissue boxes
instead of drums, taping mics to the studio floor and doing push-
ups while singing, recording in the bathroom, turning knobs 180
degrees from where they'd been set by the engineers ... Lindsey
was under severe stress in his efforts to produce something so
different that no one could compare to *Rumours*.

Was he successful? Well, yes ... and no. Lindsey's new wave
approach to the production means that almost everything has
been stripped down to the bare essentials, but at least half of
the songs are still brilliant — Christine McVie's 'Over and Over',
'Think About Me', 'Never Make Me Cry' and 'Brown Eyes'
(with Peter Green playing guitar as it fades out), and Stevie
Nicks's 'Sara', 'Storms' and 'Sisters of the Moon'. Lindsey's
contributions take a little more time to get your head around
but, the more you play *Tusk*, the more it kind of gets under your
skin.

Just like the Beatles' 'White Album', double albums like this need
more space, more room to breathe, more time to mature before
they can really be judged meaningfully. Despite its perception as
a flop by Warner Bros at a cost of $1.4million, it is now seen by
some as a masterpiece. How times change. What do I think? Is
it up there with the Beatles' 'White Album', the Rolling Stones'
Exile on Main Street? Jimi Hendrix's *Electric Ladyland*? Bob
Dylan's *Blonde on Blonde*? No. But a very good effort.

(*The Alternate Tusk* was released as part of the *Tusk* [Deluxe]
boxset in 2015 and as a limited edition of 5,000 vinyl copies on
Record Store Day in 2016, offering very different mixes of the
same songs. Not easy to find but well worth a listen.)

MIRAGE

1982

PRODUCER: Lindsey Buckingham, Ken Caillat, Richard Dashut
and Fleetwood Mac
RECORDED: Le Chateau d'Herouville, France, Larrabee Sound
Studios and the Record Plant, Los Angeles
UK: No. 5
USA: No. 1

The first Fleetwood Mac LP to be recorded outside of the UK or
USA and the first release after a three-year wait, *Mirage* did well
in the UK and US charts but was regarded by just about everyone
except devout fans as dull and disappointing: "wispy nonsense"
was how Richard Cook of the *New Musical Express* described it.

The frustrating thing is that there's not really a bad song on this LP, but neither are there any stand-out tracks either, except Stevie Nick's 'Gypsy', which she held over for this album in memory of her best friend, Robin Snyder, who had sadly passed away in 1982.

The first three numbers drift along dreamily — one each from Christine McVie, Lindsey Buckingham and Stevie Nicks — but it's not until the fourth number, 'Book of Love' by Lindsey and producer Richard Dashut, that things really get moving.

Christine McVie's first song is 'Only Over You', followed by 'Hold Me' on side two — both songs influenced by her partner Dennis Wilson from the Beach Boys, from whom she had recently split and who, sadly, would die 18 months later. Both are decent numbers but lack any real hooks and suffer terribly from the '80s curse of drum programming and over-prominent bass. 'Stand Back' by Stevie struggles with the same problem.

Lindsey's numbers — 'Empire State' and 'Eyes of the World' are the two that come closest to *Tusk* and are welcome for it in terms of energy levels, while his other success was 'Oh Diane', a '50s parody that made it to the Top 10 in the UK, perhaps influenced by Shakin' Stevens's No. 1 smash hit, 'The Green Door', the year before.

Pretty much everything on Mirage is lacking in passion and intensity and suffers far more from poor production than poor songwriting. The cover artwork sums things up. While the *Tusk* cover looked violent, aggressive and interesting, this looks (and sounds) like an '80s clothes catalogue for middle-aged, middle class commuters who like nothing better than strolling along the middle of the road.

A bit harsh and we must remember it is the '80s and nothing sounded much different to this. With better production and some decent promotion, *Mirage* could have done better and been much more fondly remembered.

(*The Alternate Mirage* was released as part of the *Mirage* [Deluxe] boxset in 2016 and as a limited edition of 3,500 vinyl copies on Record Store Day in 2017, offering early alternate versions of the same songs.)

TANGO IN THE NIGHT

1987

PRODUCER: Lindsey Buckingham and Richard Dashut
RECORDED: Rumbo Recorders and the Slope, Los Angeles
UK: No. 1
USA: No. 7

A tricky one this. So many people consider this the second best Fleetwood Mac album, with only *Rumours* topping the bill above it. That can only be considered if you don't include any of the pre-Buckingham/Nicks LPs, that's for sure. But of the later albums, there are several I prefer to this, despite the fact it includes some great numbers that wouldn't have been out of place on *Rumours*.

Lindsey Buckingham's opening 'Big Love' kicks things off superbly, followed by Stevie Nicks's 'Seven Wonders' and Christine McVie's 'Everywhere' — not a bad opening 11 minutes for any LP, created once again during a period of despair and disarray among the band. All except John McVie had been working on solo projects and all were suffering from personal problems, disruption, addictions, financial issues and even tragedies. It was up to Lindsey to persuade them to stumble into the studio to have another go.

Stevie Nicks wasn't overly keen, given that she was battling against cocaine and alcohol addictions in the Betty Ford Center and working hard to promote her solo LP, *Rock A Little*. Her other contributions, though, are pretty good — 'Welcome to the Room … Sara' being an account of her time at the clinic, while the closing song 'When I See You Again' is a nice ballad in which her vocals sound much stronger and Lindsey adds some great guitar.

Lindsey contributes one more strong number, the title song 'Tango in the Night' with some decent drum patterns from Mick and Lindsey's blistering guitar solo. But now take a listen to his other two numbers, 'Family Man' (sounds suspiciously like the UK fictional singer-songwriter John Shuttleworth), while the closing number 'You and I, Part II' is even worse. Was he trying to be funny? Because he almost succeeds.

It's down to Christine McVie to rescue *Tango in the Night* with the classic 'Little Lies', co-written with husband Eddy Quintela, as is 'Isn't it Midnight', an '80s rocker in the style of Huey Lewis's 'Power of Love'. Again, that's where the problem with *Tango in the Night* lies, just as it did with *Mirage*: production values of the '80s. Too much drum programming and lacking in musical subtlety. Less is more. Drop the dross and lift the best numbers from *Mirage*, and have another go at the production, and you could have a Fleetwood Mac album that would have been worth waiting eight years for. Seven out of 12 isn't good enough.

and Billy — but all of the others are rather bland. There's one other decent song from Billy and co-writer David Malloy, called 'In the Back of My Mind', which starts off like the soundtrack to some sci-fi movie, but that's about it. Listenable, forgettable.

To be fair to the late Greg Ladanyi (who sadly was killed in a stage accident at a gig in Cyprus in 2009), his production work and overall sound was pretty good even if, again, of its time as the '80s moved into the '90s. But this is an album that most Fleetwood Mac fans probably played once or twice and then filed away.

BEHIND THE MASK

1990

PRODUCER: Greg Ladanyi and Fleetwood Mac
RECORDED: The Complex, Los Angeles and Vintage Recorders, Phoenix
UK: No. 1
USA: No. 18

Goodbye Lindsey, goodbye Richard Dashut, hello Rick Vito on lead guitar, Billy Burnette on rhythm and Greg Ladanyi in charge of production. Ladanyi had begun his career as an engineer but switched to production in the early '80s, working with the likes of Jackson Browne, Toto and Stevie's ex-partner, Don Henley.

Billy Burnette and Rick Vito had proved themselves excellent replacements for Buckingham — both excellent guitarists and songwriters — but neither really fitted the bill for Fleetwood Mac, so it doesn't really sound like them at all. More like Bryan Adams with a bit of REM and the Beatles topped off with Gilbert O'Sullivan. Not joking — take a listen to Billy Burnette's 'Hard Feelings'. Square pegs in round holes. Pleasant songs, but all just a bit forgettable when compared to Fleetwood Mac at their best. (Lindsey Buckingham does contribute some acoustic guitar on the title track.)

The problem is not Rick Vito and Billy Burnette's contributions, but the lack of input from Christine and Stevie. Both have contributed some decent numbers —the country rock 'Love is Dangerous' from Stevie and Rick, and lovely ballad 'Do You Know' from Christine

TIME

1995

PRODUCER: Fleetwood Mac, Richard Dashut, John Jones and Ray Kennedy
RECORDED: Ocean Way Recording and Sunset Sound Recorders, Hollywood
UK: No. 47
USA: Did not chart

If we complained about the lack of input from Christine and Stevie in *Behind the Mask*, this album offers even less because, by this time, Stevie had also left Fleetwood Mac. In her place came Bekka Bramlett, the 25-year-old daughter of the superb husband-and-wife country soul duo Delaney & Bonnie, and Dave Mason, former guitarist and songwriter with the British band, Traffic. Billy Burnette was still there (although he had left in 1993 to record his own solo album, *Coming Home*, but it sold very few copies and he asked to return), while Rick Vito had left to make an album with Stevie. Swings and roundabouts, once again.

A lot of Fleetwood Mac fans loathe this album and slate it remorselessly, which is understandable, but it's preferable to *Behind the Mask*, especially if you like Delaney & Bonnie and country blues, whoever's playing. Bekka has a good voice and the album kicks off with a great Billy Burnette song, 'Talkin' to My Heart', which she sings really well. Great to hear Mick Fleetwood and John McVie back in their place as a proper rhythm section as well, after all that silly '80s stuff.

RIGHT

Christine McVie and her husband Eddy Quintela's first number 'Hollywood (Some Other Kind of Town)' is also very good. In fact, Christine and Eddy contribute five songs to this album, all of which are very listenable. We also have a good country rocker 'Nothing Without You' co-written by Bekka with her father, Delaney Bramlett, and Nashville songwriter Doug Gilmore (some backing vocals from Lindsey Buckingham on this number, too). Bekka also sings her ballad, co-written with Billy Burnette, 'Dreamin' the Dream', beautifully well.

There are no bad songs on *Time* except, possibly, Mick Fleetwood's 'These Strange Times', which certainly is a little strange. What you've got here is a decent album from a tight little country blues band, half-performed by Christine McVie (who happens to be in Fleetwood Mac) and half by Bekka Bramlett (who happens to be the daughter of Delaney & Bonnie). And great performances by a backing band made up of four terrific musicians. What's not to like? It's just not Fleetwood Mac. But worth a listen.

SAY YOU WILL

2003

PRODUCER: Lindsey Buckingham, Rob Cavallo and John Shanks
RECORDED: The Bellagio House, Ocean Way Recording, Lindsey's garage and Cornerstone Recording Studios, Los Angeles
UK: No. 6
USA: No. 73

There was an eight-year wait between *Time* and *Say You Will*, proving the point that sometimes it's worth waiting a few more years for something worth having. Even without Christine McVie (except for two songs intended for Lindsey's solo album, on which she supplied keyboards and vocals) this is the best Fleetwood Mac album since *Tusk*. Just like *Tusk*, you could argue that a double CD with 18 tracks is a bridge too far. But eight years are

eight years, and there was an awful lot of material, half of it written by Lindsey Buckingham, that needed making use of. This is dominated by Lindsey's songs and production, but Stevie is back with some terrific songs as well and certainly not under his shadow as she had been on *Tango in the Night*.

Lindsey's opener 'What's the World Coming To' (co-written with Julian Raymond — producer and songwriter for Glen Campbell and Cheap Trick, among others) — kind of typifies the overall sound of this album — very much country rock indie pop with tones of R.E.M., Counting Crows, the Jayhawks, Wilco et al, but who influenced who? Does it matter? This album is a commitment at 76 minutes, but it's worth it and gets better each time.

Track two is also Lindsey's, 'Murrow Turning Over in His Grave' with a gutsy guitar solo of a level of energy we hadn't heard from him in a long time. That's followed by two decent songs from Stevie leaning towards country rock, especially 'Thrown Down' — one of her best songs. Then two more equally impressive numbers from Lindsey — 'Miranda' and 'Red Rover' — both with some superb guitar work, great harmonies, and the sort of rhythm section performance from Mick and John that we haven't heard from them in a long time, either.

Next, a jolly little folk singalong from Stevie, the title track 'Say You Will', with vocal backup from some of the band's own children or relatives — the happiest Fleetwood Mac song, probably ever; 'Peacekeeper' from Lindsey — R.E.M. influenced or I'll eat my hat; 'Come', the heaviest song since 'Oh Well' back in Peter Green days. It all sounds too good to be true but they maintain that standard, or close to it, pretty much all the way through.

Negatives? In reality, just a Buckingham-Nicks album? Yes, but that's not a disaster, and Mick and John's contribution shouldn't be undervalued. Does it miss any songs from Christine McVie? Yes, but not so much that it's any less impressive. Too long? Yes, but they knew anything dropped might never get another chance. Over-produced and harmonised? Yes, a little, but this is Fleetwood Mac. If *Say You Will* is their swansong, it's not a bad one to leave us with.

STUDIO ALBUMS
FROM WORST TO BEST

17. BEHIND THE MASK

1990

Lindsey Buckingham has departed and the result is an album that's bland and instantly forgettable. Move on.

16. PENGUIN

1973

Some decent material from Bob Welch and Christine McVie but the new line-up struggled to gel, resulting in fillers and a lack of direction.

15. KILN HOUSE

1970

A split between rock 'n' roll parodies from Jeremy Spencer and some nice, ethereal songs from Danny Kirwan results in an LP that's totally disjointed.

14. TIME

1995

Actually not a bad album, especially if you like country blues in the style of Delaney & Bonnie, but not really Fleetwood Mac.

13. MR WONDERFUL

1968

In effect a live performance in the studio but not very well produced and too many Elmore James parodies from Jeremy Spencer.

12. BARE TREES

1972

Continues where *Future Games* left off but loses its way a little, despite some decent material.

11. TANGO IN THE NIGHT

1987

Am I the only one who finds this disappointing? Spoiled by '80s production values and a couple of turkeys, this should otherwise be up in the top 5.

10. HEROES ARE HARD TO FIND

1974

Bob Welch's farewell LP with Fleetwood Mac is potentially great but runs out of steam towards the end. Nonetheless, a step in the right direction.

9. MIRAGE

1982

Also suffers from '80s production values but includes some great songs, even if it lacks a little energy and tends to cruise along the middle of the road.

8. MYSTERY TO ME

1973

Basically a Bob Welch/Christine McVie-dominated LP that is remarkable good, despite wide cracks spreading through the band's personal relationships.

7. SAY YOU WILL

2003

Surprisingly good, despite no Christine McVie and rather too long. No bad tracks, it's Fleetwood Mac's most mellow album, even when covering darker themes.

6. [PETER GREEN'S] FLEETWOOD MAC

1968

Where it all began in 1967 — one of the best blues albums to come out of the '60s British blues explosion.

5. THEN PLAY ON

1969

The best of Peter Green's three LPs with Fleetwood Mac, and sadly his last, but makes a move away from pure blues towards something a little more interesting.

4. FUTURE GAMES

1971

Bob Welch and Christine McVie join the band and reveal their songwriting talents for the first time as they drift effortlessly towards softer, '70s, West Coast rock.

3. TUSK

1979

Experimental, radical, disparate and hated by many when released but now regarded as something of a masterpiece, if slightly bonkers.

2. FLEETWOOD MAC [WHITE ALBUM]

1975

Created within six months from the day Buckingham/Nicks met Fleetwood/McVie/McVie, this was the blueprint for the future of Fleetwood Mac.

1. RUMOURS

1977

Would anyone disagree this should be No. 1? The result of three brilliant songwriters working under the influence of pain, misery, despair and lots of drink and drugs. Perfect.

RIGHT

Rumours sleeve design

A SELECTION OF THE BEST COMPILATIONS & LIVE ALBUMS

ENGLISH ROSE

1969 USA ONLY

A compilation for the US market only combining non-LP singles and *Mr Wonderful*.

THE PIOUS BIRD OF GOOD OMEN

1969 UK ONLY

UK compilation of A- and B-sides from early singles and various album tracks.

BLUES JAM AT CHESS

1969

Fleetwood Mac contributed to the jam sessions at the Chess Ter-Mar Studios in Chicago with Otis Spann, Willie Dixon, Walter 'Shakey' Horton, J.T. Brown, Buddy Guy, David 'Honey Boy' Edwards and S.P. Leary. The recordings were released as *Blues Jam at Chess* in December 1969 and are now available on CDs as *Blues Jam in Chicago, Volumes 1 and 2*.)

GREATEST HITS

1971

Superb compilation album that combines all the singles plus a couple of the best tracks from *Mr Wonderful*.

LIVE

1980

Recorded during the *Tusk* world tour in Japan, France, England and America, it's not the best sound quality but decent performances.

GREATEST HITS

1988

The second *Greatest Hits* album from the Buckingham-Nicks era, with the addition of two new songs performed with Rick Vito and Billy Burnette — Stevie Nicks's 'No Questions Asked' and Christine McVie and Eddy Quintela's 'As Long As You Follow'.

25 YEARS – THE CHAIN

1992

A 4-CD boxset covering the 25 years from 1967 to 1992. Includes various live versions, remixes, unreleased material and four new songs — Stevie Nicks, John Heron and Rick Vito's 'Paper Doll'; Christine McVie and Eddy Quintela's 'Love Shines' and 'Heart of Stone'; and Lindsey Buckingham's 'Make Me a Mask'. A condensed 2-CD version also available.

LIVE AT THE BBC

1995 UK ONLY

Double CD compilation of various radio sessions for the BBC between 1967 and 1971, including several tracks otherwise unavailable.

THE DANCE

1997

Recorded for an MTV *The Dance* special at Warner Bros Studios in Burbank, California, for release as a live DVD and CD. Includes the University of Southern California Trojan Marching Band on the last two numbers, 'Tusk' and 'Don't Stop'.

THE VERY BEST OF FLEETWOOD MAC

2002

A single CD compilation in the UK and a double CD version in the USA, includes various live versions, remixes and unreleased material. The US double CD version was released in the UK in 2009.

THE BEST OF PETER GREEN'S FLEETWOOD MAC

2002

Based on the 1971 *Greatest Hits* album of early material but expanded. Includes Chicken Shack's 'I'd Rather Go Blind' sung by Christine McVie.

THE ESSENTIAL FLEETWOOD MAC

2007

Comprehensive compilation of early recordings from 1967-68. Includes most of the tracks from their first two albums plus non-album singles and some rarities.

LIVE IN BOSTON
(AKA BOSTON, BOSTON LIVE, JUMPING AT SHADOWS AND LIVE AT THE BOSTON TEA PARTY)

VARIOUS RELEASE DATES FROM 1994 – 2014

Live recordings over three nights at the Boston Tea Party venue in Boston, Massachusetts, in February 1970 for a planned live album that was shelved. Various four-volume, single-volume and boxset versions available on CD and vinyl. A superb live performance of the classic early Fleetwood Mac line-up. Well-worth seeking out to hear them at their best.

LIVE IN BOSTON

2004

Same title as above but this recorded 34 years later over two nights at the FleetCenter in Boston during the *Say You Will* tour in 2003. A 10-track CD forms part of a double DVD package.

IN CONCERT

2016

Live recordings from the *Tusk* tour in 1979-80 originally released in the *Tusk* [Deluxe] Edition in 2015. Features 22 selected live performances, mostly recorded at Wembley Arena in London and the Checkerdome in St. Louis. Available as a vinyl three-LP set on 180-gram vinyl.

Acknowledgements & Sources

The following books and periodicals provided invaluable information and quotations:

BRUNNING, BOB
Blues: The British Connection (Originally published as *Blues in Britain*)

BRUNNING, BOB
The Fleetwood Mac Story: Rumours and Lies

COLEMAN, RAY
Survivor: The Authorised Biography of Eric Clapton

DIXON, WILLIE (WITH DON SNOWDON)
I Am the Blues

EGAN, SEAN (EDITOR)
Fleetwood Mac on Fleetwood Mac: Interviews & Encounters

ERLEWINE, MICHAEL (EXECUTIVE EDITOR)
All Music Guide to the Blues

EVANS, MIKE
Fleetwood Mac: The Definitive History

FLEETWOOD, MICK (WITH ANTHONY BOZZA)
Play On: Now, Then & Fleetwood Mac

FLEETWOOD, MICK (WITH STEPHEN DAVIS)
Fleetwood: My Life and Adventures with Fleetwood Mac

GORDON, ROBERT
Can't Be Satisfied: The Life and Times of Muddy Waters

GURALNICK, PETER
Feel Like Going Home: Portraits in Blues and Rock 'n' Roll

HARRIS, CAROL ANN
Storms: My Life with Lindsey Buckingham and Fleetwood Mac

HJORT, CHRISTOPHER
Strange Brew: Eric Clapton & The British Blues Boom 1965-1970

HOSKYNS, BARNEY
Waiting for the Sun: Strange Days, Weird Scenes & the Sound of Los Angeles

KNIGHT, RICHARD
Blues Highway: New Orleans to Chicago - A Travel and Music Guide

LOGOZ, DINU
John Mayall: The Blues Crusader

MCSTRAVICK, SUMMER AND ROOS, JOHN (EDITORS)
Blues-Rock Explosion

NORMAN, PHILIP
The Stones

OLDHAM, ANDREW LOOG
Stoned

OLDHAM, ANDREW LOOG
2 Stoned

ROBERTS, DAVID (EDITOR)
Guinness British Hit Singles

SCHUMACHER, MICHAEL
Crossroads: The Life and Music of Eric Clapton

TOOZE, SANDRA B.
Muddy Waters: The Mojo Man

WARD, GREG
The Rough Guide to Essential Blues CDs

WYMAN, BILL (WITH RICHARD HAVERS)
Blues Odyssey

NEWSPAPERS
Daily Mail (London)
Daily Telegraph (London)
Guardian (London)
Independent (London)
Irish Times (Dublin)
Los Angeles Times
Sunday Times (London)
Times (London)

PERIODICALS
Billboard
Blues Magazine
Classic Rock
Magnet
Melody Maker
Mojo
New Musical Express
Q
Record Mirror
Record Collector
Rolling Stone
Shindig!
Sounds
Sunday Times Magazine
Uncut

TELEVISION/VIDEO/DVD
BBC2 — *Later...With Jools Holland*
BBC4 — *Fleetwood Mac: Don't Stop*
Candlewood Films/Sanctuary 2013 — *Fleetwood Mac: Destiny Rules*
Classic Albums/Eagle Rock 2007 — *Fleetwood Mac: Rumours*
Rhino 1998 — *The Dance*
Rhino 2003 — *Tango in the Night*
Scanbox International 2007/Wienerworld 2009 — *The Peter Green Story: Man of the World*

WEB SITES
allmusic.com
billboard.com
brunningonline.net
discogs.com
fleetwoodmac.com
fleetwoodmac.net
fleetwoodmacnews.com
lindseybuckingham.com
magnetmagazine.com
mickfleetwoodofficial.com
mojo4music.com
nme.com
qthemusic.com
rockalittle.com
rockcellarmagazine.com
rollingstone.com
shindig-magazine.com
stevienicksofficial.com
teamrock.com
ultimateclassicrock.com
uncut.co.uk
warnerbrosrecords.com

For their help, advice and encouragement, many thanks to Gary O'Neill, Huw Thomas, Linda Simone, Phil McDonnell, Gerry McAvoy and Sally Beeby.

For Jamie & Kate, Liam & Jaime, Amy & Mark ... and the next generation of Fleetwood Mac fans.